FOR GIRLS only

Wise Words, Good Advice

FOR GIRLS only

Wise Words, Good Advice

CAROL WESTON

AN AVON CAMELOT BOOK

AVON BOOKS
A division of
The Hearst Corporation
1350 Avenue of the Americas
New York, New York 10019

Copyright © 1998 by Carol Weston
Published by arrangement with the author
Visit our website at **http://www.AvonBooks.com**
ISBN: 0-380-79538-8

Library of Congress Cataloging in Publication Data:

Weston, Carol.
  For girls only : wise words, good advice / Carol Weston.
      p.   cm.
Summary: Contains quotations and advice that are relevant to girls, from a wide
variety of sources on topics such as friendship, love, and self-esteem.
1. Conduct of life—Quotations, maxims, etc.   2. Girls—Conduct of life.   [1. Conduct of life—Quotations, maxims, etc.   2. Quotations.]   I. Title
PN6084.C556W47   1997   97-30999
082—dc21   CIP
                                                                           AC

First Avon Camelot Printing: April 1998

CAMELOT TRADEMARK REG. U.S. PAT. OFF. AND IN OTHER COUNTRIES, MARCA REGISTRADA,
HECHO EN U.S.A.

Printed in the U.S.A.

OPM   10   9   8   7   6   5   4   3   2   1

For Elizabeth and Emme

Acknowledgments

To Elise Howard for having the best idea ever.

To my family, especially Robert Weston Ackerman, editor extraordinaire; Mark Weston, quote finder; and Marybeth Weston Lobdell, who read the whole manuscript, pencil in hand, the day before deadline.

To Matilde Reategui, Kyla Brennan, Maureen Davison, Laurel Davis, Molly Woodroofe, Hannah Judy, and Sue Hipkins. And also to my book club and to the friends who sustain me.

To fellow collectors of proverbs and quotations, including Robert Masello, Mary Biggs, Barbara Rowes, J. M. and M. J. Cohen, Karl Petit, Bergen Evans, and John Bartlett.

And to the many women and men who spoke and wrote so quotably in the first place.

Thank you!

Contents

Introduction

The beginning is the most important part of the work.

Plato

When I was a girl I loved quotation books. I waded through volume after volume looking for lines that spoke to me. What I found were great men's words on war, honor, death. What I wanted was good advice on love, friendship, pimples. And while I dog-eared Ben Franklin, Mark Twain, and Oscar Wilde, I also wanted to hear from women. And Asians. And African-Americans.

For Girls Only is a book of wisdom and inspiration. I selected hundreds of quotations relevant to girls, then added my own spin. You'll find lines from Aesop and Buddha, Colette and Confucius, Dear Abby and Dr. Seuss, Socrates and Seinfeld, Maya Lin and Maya Angelou, Anne Frank and Oprah Winfrey. Not to mention Ben Franklin, Mark Twain, and Oscar Wilde.

Martha Washington said, "The greater part of our happiness or misery depends on our disposition and not on our circumstances." I believe you can improve your attitude and yourself—especially when you're young—and I also believe you can learn to live more thoughtfully and happily. I hope this book can serve as a compass and guide, as well as an introduction to some of the world's most wonderful voices.

A few quotations will seem to contradict each other because even folk wisdom can't straighten out life's twists and turns. ("A proverb," wrote Miguel de Cervantes, "is a short sentence based on long experience.") Yes, slow and steady wins the race. But the early bird still gets the worm.

Might boys enjoy this book? Absolutely. But, as always, I write for girls. I've been writing for girls ever since, at age nineteen, I wrote for *Seventeen*, then later wrote the first edition of my first book, *Girltalk*. Who knew that eventually *Girltalk* would be translated into Chinese and Russian and that I'd have daughters of my own?

As you read *For Girls Only*, you may want to flip through, pausing on pages that catch your eye or searching for the quote you need for your essay or letter or yearbook. Or you may want to heed the words of Lewis Carroll, who wrote, "Begin at the beginning, and go on till you come to the end: then stop." The very last pages are blank—they await your own favorite quips and quotations.

Is it possible to distill the wisdom of the ages into one slim volume? No. Even the best mix of bons mots would fall short. But it was fun to try. And to quote Steve Martin: "I think I did pretty well considering I started out with nothing but a bunch of blank paper."

You You You

To love oneself is the beginning of a lifelong romance.

Oscar Wilde

Love yourself. Love the things that make you you. Your values and talents and memories. Your clothes, your nose, your woes. If you love yourself, you can jump into your life from a springboard of self-confidence. If you love yourself, you can say what you want to say, go where you want to go.

The world can be a tough place, and some of the billions of people out there will try to knock you down. Don't join them. Do things that make you proud, then take pride in what you do. And in who you are.

Who are you anyway? What makes you you? How are you like your siblings and neighbors and friends? How are you different? If you were your secret admirer, what would you most admire?

"My great mistake, the fault for which I can't forgive myself," Oscar Wilde wrote, "is that one day I ceased my obstinate pursuit of my own individuality." Keep pursuing your individuality. Keep being yourself. Becoming yourself. It can be comforting to dress and act like everyone else. But it is grander to be different, to be unique, to be you.

I'm the only me in the whole wide world.

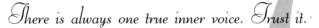

There is always one true inner voice. Trust it.

Gloria Steinem

Sometimes it's hard to know who you are and what you want and whom you like and why you like that person. The answers change because you're changing. Growing.

But deep inside, you are you. You were you as a baby, you were you as a kid, and you are you right now.

"Let me listen to me and not to them," wrote Gertrude Stein. It makes sense to consider the advice and opinions of other people. But don't let their noise drown out your inner voice. And don't let the way you sometimes talk or behave in front of others make you lose sight of who you are when you are alone, when you are most you.

"You can live a lifetime and, at the end of it, know more about other people than you know about yourself," aviator Beryl Markham cautioned. Get acquainted with yourself. Tune in to the dreams you have by day and by night. Blend in when you choose to, but appreciate the qualities that set you apart.

Anybody can be one of the crowd.

Being a teenager is a confusing time. That's the lovely thing that happens as you grow older: You are more confident and more loving of yourself. It's easier to say, "You know, that's just not me."

Vanessa Williams

It takes years to discover who you are and to understand the rules of the game. Years to figure out how to be loyal to yourself and respectful of others. Tom Cruise said, "I truly believe high school is just about the toughest time in anyone's life." The good news: Confidence is cumulative. As Alanis Morissette sings: "You live, you learn."

Adolescents and adults have always had difficulty appreciating each other. Here's what Socrates wrote way back in 400 B.C.: "Young people nowadays love luxury; they have bad manners and contempt for authority. They show disrespect for old people . . . contradict their parents, talk constantly in front of company, gobble their food and tyrannize their teachers."

Some strife is inevitable. But harmony and respect between generations is still a worthy and attainable goal.

*No wonder I go up and down—
these are roller-coaster years.*

One is not born a woman—one becomes one.

Simone de Beauvoir

Some girls are in a mad rush to develop; others want to stay kids forever. Eventually everyone reaches puberty, but it can be a time when, according to Simone de Beauvoir, girls "stop being and start seeming." Do you know girls who, instead of being themselves, are always impersonating others? Posing and posturing and playing dress-up full-time?

It can be hard to stay true to yourself when you also want to be like your friends. Hard to figure out where they stop and you start. Becoming an individual doesn't happen overnight, and you can't be introspective on the run. Walt Whitman wrote, "I loaf and invite my soul." And: "I contradict myself? Very well then I contradict myself. (I am large. I contain multitudes.)" If you act differently with different people, it doesn't mean you're a hopeless hypocrite. It means that you're still finding out who you are—and also that you're sensitive enough to be aware not just of your mouth but of others' ears.

I am discovering who I am.

*Know thyself? If I knew myself,
I'd run away.*

Goethe

Of course, you have moments of self-doubt. A person who never suffers from self-doubt may be arrogant and insufferable. But to constantly second-guess or berate or feel sorry for yourself is not ideal, either. "Self-pity in its early stages is as snug as a feather mattress," said Oprah Winfrey. "Only when it hardens does it become uncomfortable."

Forgive yourself for not being perfect, then strive to shore up your shortcomings. Can you be a more considerate friend, sister, granddaughter? Can you work harder at flute, math, or helping others? Can you step out from behind the curtain of shyness or sloth? Can you realize your potential?

Dorothy Parker wrote:

*I shall stay the way I am
Because I do not give a damn.*

Good poem; bad attitude. A little effort goes a long way. And if you start out apathetic, you can wind up pathetic.

Step-by-step, I can move forward.

This little light of mine, I'm gonna let it shine.

African-American spiritual

If you diss yourself, others will follow. If you believe in yourself, others will follow.

When you strut your stuff, you're not being a show-off. You're making a contribution. Sharing your gifts. It takes courage to get out of your own way and run with your talents. Courage to excel in something. But don't you owe it to yourself to succeed?

"There's only one corner of the universe you can be certain of improving and that's your own self," wrote Aldous Huxley. Keep learning and reaching and shining. Keep respecting and improving yourself. Madeleine L'Engle, author of *A Wrinkle in Time*, put it this way: "I do not think I will ever reach a stage when I will say, 'This is what I believe. Finished.' What I believe is alive and open to growth."

Though fools may never change their minds, wise people do. You can always see things in new ways. You can always stretch yourself. You're not done till you're dead.

I am a work in progress.

The real fault is to have faults and not amend them.

Confucius

A Hindu proverb says, "There is nothing noble about being superior to some other person. The true nobility is in being superior to your previous self." How have you grown this year? (Besides in height.) What have you learned in school? (Besides some history.) Have you taken a step forward in athletics or academics or art? Or have you learned, perhaps, that when you argue, your words have more impact if spoken quietly?

"Criticism," wrote Eleanor Roosevelt, "makes very little dent upon me, unless I think there is some real justification and something should be done." If a jerk insults you, shrug it off. Why let a jerk bring you down? But if someone you admire points out that you could have done better, don't let the words hurt you. Learn from them. Criticism stings most when you recognize truth in it. Yet in everybody and everything there is room for improvement. Instead of being defensive, reach higher, work harder. "Happy are they," wrote Shakespeare, "that hear their detractions and can put them to mending."

Thoughtful criticism can be a favor in disguise.

*One should examine oneself for a very long time
before thinking of condemning others.*

Molière

Are you too critical? Do you routinely find fault in your best friend's clothes or hair or oral report or taste in boys? Do you flip through magazines and point out how terrible every woman looks, or channel surf and comment on how stupid every actor sounds? It's one thing to develop style and standards. It's another to make cynicism your specialty.

In *The Portrait of a Lady* by Henry James, Isabel Archer defends her friend: "It is very easy to laugh at her, but it is not as easy to be as brave as she." Exactly. It's a cinch to poke fun at someone in the spotlight, a challenge to step into the glare yourself. So why not be generous? You don't have to give a standing ovation to everyone who makes a speech or sings a solo or writes an editorial. But why be mean-spirited—unless you would have others judge you as harshly? As Winston Churchill's mother, Jennie Jerome Churchill, wrote, "Treat your friends as you do your pictures, and place them in their best light."

Supportive beats sarcastic.

10

I don't know the key to success, but the key to failure is trying to please everybody.

Bill Cosby

Try to please yourself—not the indifferent popular group or your fickle friends or your impatient boyfriend or your unreasonable father.

"I was raised to sense what someone wanted me to be, and be that kind of person," actress Sally Field recalls. "It took me a long time not to judge myself through someone else's eyes."

It is tempting to let others judge you, tempting to ask "What do you think?" as you put on an outfit or sketch a portrait or play a tune or create a home page. And true experts can offer valuable guidance. Yet many classmates and grown-ups know less than you do about your fields of interest. So don't listen to them. Listen to the YES inside yourself. Give yourself a green light.

A Danish proverb says it like this: "He who builds according to every man's advice will have a crooked house."

If I do things their way, who will do things my way?

Keep in mind always the present you are constructing. It should be the future you want.

Alice Walker

Are you looking ahead? You have time to figure out where you are going and which doors to push open when you get there.

"A woman can do anything," wrote Barbara Walters. "She can be traditionally feminine and that's all right; she can work, she can stay at home; she can be aggressive, she can be passive; she can be any way she wants with a man. But whenever there are the kinds of choices there are today, unless you have some solid base, life can be frightening."

Everyone gets overwhelmed, but there's no need to be frightened. Variety and vitality are among the privileges of youth. And you can sign up for courses and activities that will help you explore different paths and fields just as you can look for mentors and peers who share your interests. You can build your base and your future.

This is the time of my life.

To keep the body in good health is a duty.

Buddha

*A*re you taking good care of yourself, body and soul, inside and outside? Buddha may have had a spare tire, but he was right about the importance of health.

"The field that has rested gives a beautiful crop," wrote Ovid. It is hard to turn off the lights when life feels full, but getting enough sleep is one key to staying healthy and happy. If you drink cola with dinner and then stay up until dawn chatting on-line, you'll be wiped out the next day. Instead, snuggle into bed with or without a book. Nab that beauty sleep. They say breaking up is hard to do, but waking up can be even harder—especially when you're sleep-deprived.

Get enough exercise, too. Whether you run, bicycle, skate, rollerblade, or snowboard, whether you work out alone or with a team, staying fit means staying healthy. "Nothing lifts me out of a bad mood better than a hard workout," wrote Cher. "Exercise is nothing short of a miracle."

I have only one body.
I had better take care of it.

13

At thirteen, I thought more about my acne than I did about God or world peace.

Mary Pipher

You get to make a first impression only once. Yet just when you want to look your most dazzling, you have to contend with pimples or braces or the terrible awkwardness of maturing more quickly or slowly than your friends. Everyone feels insecure at this age—especially the people who boast most. The challenge is to smile as you make it through the obstacle course of adolescence.

"Perhaps because her bite is worse than her admittedly formidable bark, Miss Manners is in sympathy with people who wear braces on their teeth," Judith Martin wrote. "However," she added, "refusing to smile for two and a half years does nothing at all for one's social standing."

Enthusiasm makes you attractive no matter what your skin, teeth, or body is up to. So don't just fixate on the physical. Smile. And take comfort: Acne is not a losing battle, because you win in the end.

I don't notice everyone else's new zits; why would they notice mine?

I think women see me on the cover of magazines and think I never have a pimple or bags under my eyes. You have to realize that that's after two hours of hair and makeup, plus retouching. Even I don't wake up looking like Cindy Crawford.

Cindy Crawford

You can try to look your best. You can wash your hair and brush your teeth. You can even apply makeup. But be reasonable. In real life, supermodels don't look like supermodels. And since you probably don't expect to sing as well as your favorite musician or run as fast as well as your favorite athlete, why despair just because you and a cover girl don't look like twins separated at birth?

"Zest is the secret of all beauty," said Christian Dior. "Good posture is the one thing anybody can do now to look better," wrote Helen Gurley Brown. Zeal and self-confidence really are more attractive than perfect hair or perfect skin. So repeat after María in *West Side Story*: "I feel pretty, oh so pretty . . . "

When I feel good, I look good.

I didn't belong as a kid, and that always bothered me. If only I'd known that one day my differences would be an asset, then my early life would have been much easier.

Bette Midler

It's hard to feel awesome when you feel awkward. But hang in there. Believe in yourself; befriend yourself; be patient.

Remember *The Ugly Duckling*? Remember the happy ending? "He thought of how he had been taunted and tormented, and now he heard all of them saying that he was the most beautiful of all beautiful birds," wrote Hans Christian Andersen. "He ruffled his feathers and lifted his slender neck, and from his heart he sang: 'I never dreamed of this much happiness when I was the ugly duckling.'"

You can't skip adolescence. But would you really want to? As Emily Dickinson wrote:

That it will never come again
Is what makes life so sweet.

I won't just be self-conscious;
I will be conscious of my self.

Clothes are the mirror of the soul, and your soul, as you know, is multifaceted, multileveled, and too complex for words. You can't stick to one look when one second you feel like Emily Dickinson and the next like Bette Midler.

Cynthia Heimel

While some girls may be predictable or one-dimensional, you may like all sorts of clothes, books, foods, people.

What do your clothes say about you? Gilda Radner joked, "I base most of my fashion taste on what doesn't itch." Clothes don't have to be new or name brand. Why not wear what makes you feel comfortable, whether that means chic and pulled together, loose and laid-back, or a mix, depending on the week or the whim? Slowly, slowly dare to wear clothes that help tell people who you are.

Do you have style? "Oh, you've got to have style! It helps you get up in the morning!" said Diana Vreeland. If you like the way someone looks or dresses, ask yourself why. Train your eye and experiment with jewelry, accessories, fabrics, color. "There is no such thing as an ugly woman—there are only the ones who do not know how to make themselves attractive," said Christian Dior.

I can put color in my life.

Women should try to increase their size rather than decrease it, because I believe the bigger we are, the more space we'll take up, and the more we'll have to be reckoned with.

Roseanne

That's one approach. But truth is, it's healthier to be fit than fat. Miguel de Cervantes, author of *Don Quixote*, was the first to ask, "Can we ever have too much of a good thing?" When it comes to food, the answer is yes. Being comfortable with yourself and your size is an important goal. But constant overeating may mean that something is bothering you—something is "eating" you.

Many girls get obsessed by weight. But although eating too much can make you chubby, eating too little is just as bad. Skipping meals leaves you hungry and deprives your body of necessary energy and nutrients. And starving yourself or throwing up on purpose is downright dangerous. So rather than count calories or go on wacky diets or hop on the scale each day, cut back on seconds, snacks, and soda, and eat sensible balanced meals. As Molière said, "One should eat to live, not live to eat." Don't let food run—or ruin—your life.

Eating healthfully shows self-respect.

18

Manners are the happy way of doing things.

Ralph Waldo Emerson

"Your manners are always under examination," wrote Emerson, "and are awarding or denying you very high prizes when you least think of it."

You may grumble when your grandmother says "Napkin on your lap" or "Elbows off the table" or "Start with the outside fork," but people do notice your manners—as much as your appearance. Even cavemen munching mastodons probably followed some sort of protocol.

Have you ever heard this poem by Gelett Bergess?

> *The Goops they lick their fingers,*
> *And the Goops they lick their knives;*
> *They spill their broth on the tablecloth—*
> *Oh, they lead disgusting lives!*
> *The Goops they talk while eating,*
> *And loud and fast they chew;*
> *And that is why I'm glad that I*
> *Am not a Goop—are you?*

Manners matter.

Women understand the world more than men, therefore they weep more often.

The Cabala

"Though the sex to which I belong is considered weak," Queen Elizabeth I wrote a long time ago, "you will nevertheless find me a rock that bends to no wind." Women are strong. Now more than ever, thanks to the work of those who came before, women can vote, make decisions, pursue careers, and enjoy the same rights and options as men. Are women and men the same? No. But, as the French say, *"Vive la différence."*

Women derive much of their strength from their keen awareness of relationships as well as goals. "True strength is delicate," wrote sculptor Louise Nevelson.

"In passing," wrote Nancy Astor, "I would like to say that the first time Adam had a chance, he laid the blame on woman."

There may be times when you will feel you are being treated unfairly. Defend yourself. Speak your mind.

*So I cried—
it's better to be sensitive than unfeeling.*

Excellence is the best deterrent to racism or sexism.

Oprah Winfrey

f you think you're being slighted because of your sex, race, or background, you have legitimate grounds for complaint. But don't make the victim card your ace in the hole. A better approach is to pour your energy into doing your best. When you triumph, you not only come out ahead, you also have the pleasure of proving skeptics wrong.

You are writing your own "personal suspense novel," said Mary Higgins Clark. "The plot is what you will do for the rest of your life, and you are the protagonist." Why not give your story character, adventure, and a heroine who is unstoppable?

"If you are going to think black, think positive about it," wrote opera singer Leontyne Price. "Don't think down on it, or think it is something in your way. This way, when you really want to stretch out, and express how beautiful black is, everybody will hear you."

Being an individual means taking pride in my differences, my similarities, my strengths.

Where you lead, I will follow.

Carole King

*A*re you a leader or a follower or a bit of both? Steamrollers get their way—but they crush everything in their path. Followers do what the group does—but they may notice later that they've been led astray. If you are savvy and can think for yourself, you can sometimes follow other people's trails and sometimes leave a trail of your own.

Whom would you be willing to follow? Some lucky girls find mentors—teachers or older classmates who can guide them toward interesting summers or promising careers. Less lucky girls can fall in with the wrong crowd—and wind up smoking, drinking, or worse. In the Bible, Matthew wrote, "If the blind lead the blind, both shall fall in the ditch." If someone offers you cigarettes or beer or drugs, can you say no? If any group urges you to surrender your independence in order to belong, can you move on to a group where your opinions and your individuality are respected? Never get in the backseat if you don't know where you're going.

If it doesn't feel right, it might be wrong.

22

Smoking is a custom loathesome to the eye, hateful to the nose, harmful to the brain, dangerous to the lungs.

James I

The newspapers keep reporting new studies that link smoking and disease. Duh! It's not news that smoking is bad news. England's King James I figured that one out four centuries ago!

Why start smoking? It's unhealthy, addictive, smelly, and expensive. And while a few people may think you're cool if you light up, a lot of others—girls and guys—will think less of you. Cigarettes can make many would-be friendships and romances go up in smoke.

What do you do if someone offers you a puff at the bus stop or in the girls' room? Don't jump on a soapbox. Just decline. If you want, you can say that you don't like the taste or that smoking gives you a headache or that you're allergic. The point is not to start smoking. It makes your clothes smell and your teeth yellow and your lungs black and your breath gross. It can cause diseases that can kill you. It costs hundreds of dollars a year. And it's a very hard habit to break.

Start smoking? I don't think so.

One reason I don't drink is I want to know when I'm having a good time.

Nancy Astor

At some point, you may have a friend who swills a beer after school or at a party and who wants you to drink, too. It can be difficult to say no to a friend. But saying no to her or him can mean saying yes to yourself.

Drinking can be dangerous. Drinking can lead you to do something you'll later regret. Mixing drinks or drinking too much can make you throw up or pass out. Driving while drunk can cause a fatal accident. Never, ever, drive drunk—and never, ever, let someone who is drunk drive you anywhere. Call home or a taxi or a friend's parent. Do not risk your life because you're too embarrassed to speak up.

Just because your friend is drinking doesn't mean you have to. You don't have to report her or lecture her or dump her. Just take care of your own body and health. Don't go against your better judgment. As basketball star Kareem Abdul-Jabbar says, "If you're under twenty-one, it's a no-brainer. Don't give in to peer pressure. Don't drink."

I don't have to drink to have fun.

24

All dope can do for you is kill you . . . the long hard way. And it can kill the people you love right along with you.

Billie Holiday

D o you know someone on drugs? Do you think he's cool—or a fool? Do you feel respect for her? Or do you feel sorry for her?

Many older teens and adults have self-destructive habits. They smoke and find that it's hard to quit. They drink and don't know when enough is enough. They do drugs and stop paying attention to their work or friends or family. Their habits are bad for them and can be dangerous to those who love them.

The easiest way not to get addicted to a drug or not to get busted by the police because of drugs is to stay away from drugs in the first place. You don't need them.

As entertainer Arsenio Hall put it: "If God wanted us high, He would have given us wings."

Hugs, not drugs.

The plant is blind but it knows enough to keep pushing upwards towards the light, and it will do this in the face of endless discouragements.

George Orwell

If you keep forging ahead, you get where you are going. If you keep moving despite the odds and obstacles, you win. And when you do encounter hard times? Have faith that life gets easier once you get the hang of it. Experience teaches perspective; peace comes after pain; triumph can follow defeat.

"I think these difficult times have helped me to understand better than before, how infinitely rich and beautiful life is in every way," wrote Isak Dinesen, "and that so many things that one goes around worrying about are of no importance whatsoever."

To see the bigger picture, step back. That can help you distinguish major troubles from minor ones. You didn't get invited to the party? That hurts—but you still have friends. You missed an easy shot in basketball? Bummer—but you're still a good player. You have too much homework? A drag—but hey, you have food, shelter, and people who love you.

When I step back, big problems look smaller.

Two roads diverged in a wood, and I—
I took the one less traveled by,
And that has made all the difference.

Robert Frost

Take the time you need to find yourself and to find your path. You know how different you are from your friends and family and neighbors. Your passions are different, as are your successes and setbacks. Even what makes you laugh or cry may be different.

"Go confidently in the direction of your dreams!" wrote Henry David Thoreau. "Live the life you've imagined." A defender of the individual, he also wrote, "If a man does not keep pace with his companions, perhaps it is because he hears a different drummer."

If you do just what others are doing, you can wind up squooshed into a box that doesn't fit. So take charge, not orders. Answer to yourself. And consider heeding the Star Trek advice "to boldly go where no man has gone before."

If I follow the crowd,
I might get lost in it.

Friendship

My friends are my estate.
Emily Dickinson

*N*othing like good friends. They congratulate and console. They offer a sympathetic ear and a second opinion. They provide company and merriment. And they help you feel good about yourself.

You don't need one particular best friend, and you don't need to be popular. But you do need a real friend or two. As Francis Bacon put it, "Without friends, the world is but a wilderness."

Learning to be friendly and to befriend others is every bit as important as academic learning. Some girls make the mistake of competing with their friends or of becoming possessive or jealous of them. Others twist themselves into knots trying to win popularity contests. Others retreat behind shyness and live lonely lives.

Are you likeable? Do you have friends for now and friends for life?

If life is cake, friendship is frosting.

31

God gave us our relatives;
thank God we can choose our friends.

Ethel Watts Mumford

Whenever you find yourself wishing you could be friends with someone, ask yourself why. Is it because that person is pretty or popular? Or is it because you and she share common ground? With whom do you think you will have a better chance of forging a lasting friendship?

A friend is someone with whom you can think aloud. She listens with interest and without teasing. If you live to run, you might want to find a friend who wants to discuss times, tracks, and shin splints. If you love English, you might want to find a friend with whom to trade books and literary opinions. If you've weathered your parents' divorce, you might want to confide in someone whose parents have also broken up. Look for girls who share the same passions and problems and pastimes you do. Look for girls who are friendly, smart, and kind, and with whom you can relax. After all, says a French proverb, "That day is lost on which one has not laughed."

I will think about whom I want to be friends
with and why.

The only way to have a friend is to be one.

Ralph Waldo Emerson

To make friends, get involved. Join the basketball team or French club or student government or literary magazine, and meet others who share your interests. Then say hello (even if you're feeling shy) and introduce yourself. Ask questions, laugh approvingly, smile, listen well, and keep secrets.

People like people who like them. If you seem warm and interested, girls and guys will respond to you. If you say nothing, you may come off as cold and distant even if you're only timid.

Be visible and vibrant, cheerful and curious. You'll make more friends than if you spend your days inside peering wistfully out the window. Though everybody feels nervous at times, if you break through your shell you're doing yourself and those around you a favor. So try to relax. As Anne Lamott wrote, "Don't look at your feet to see if you are doing it right. Just dance."

I will get to know people;
I will let them get to know me.

33

Laugh, and the world laughs with you;
Weep, and you weep alone;
For the sad old earth must borrow its mirth,
But has trouble enough of its own.

Ella Wheeler Wilcox

*D*o you know girls who are fun and funny? Who are upbeat and enthusiastic? Who think positive and love to laugh? If so, they are probably well liked. It's hard not to like a good sport who enjoys a good time.

Being serious and earnest is admirable. Being whiny and complaining is trouble. And those who always grouse and gripe are rarely friend magnets.

"Whoever is happy will make others happy, too," wrote Anne Frank. Moods are contagious. If someone is full of vim and energy, it lifts you up. If someone is bummed out or bitter, it pulls you down. So cultivate your sense of fun. Don't conceal your zeal. Save the somber heart-to-hearts for those who already love you. As an African proverb puts it: "Sorrow is like a precious treasure shown only to friends." Friends, mind you. Not girls you just met and hope to know better.

Better sweet than sour.

You can make more friends in two months by becoming interested in other people than you can in two years by trying to get other people interested in you.

Dale Carnegie

One way to jump-start a friendship is to discover someone's passion or hobby and talk to her about it. Expressing interest in her collection of stamps, books, gemstones, earrings, political buttons, or latest CDs piques her interest in you, too. Has your classmate taken the time to put together a portfolio or a family scrapbook or to master the violin or a computer game? What would happen if you said "You're amazing!" rather than "Let's watch TV?" If you recognize and appreciate someone's talent, that person is likely to take note of your talents, too. Even if you simply ask, "How was your weekend?" before detailing the highlights of yours, that person will probably share her experiences and listen to yours with added interest.

"If therefore, there be any kindness I can show, or any good thing I can do to any fellow being," wrote William Penn, founder of Pennsylvania, the state of brotherly love, "let me do it now, and not defer or neglect it, as I shall not pass this way again."

The more generous I am with others, the more generous they may be with me.

35

Friendship is always the union of part of one mind with part of another; people are friends in spots.

George Santayana

*Y*ou may not like or agree with every word your friends say. Or you may adore them top to bottom—yet not understand one's passion for a political position or another's inability to be on time. "The art of being wise," wrote William James, "is the art of knowing what to overlook." You don't have to see eye to eye on everything or admire someone's every step. You're friends, not clones.

Do you have more than one close friend? You and one girl may like to bake together. You and a second may like to rollerblade. You and a third may like to practice your Spanish while talking about boys. (*Sí, es guapo. Es muy guapo. . . .*) It's good to have more than one friend, not just because different friends bring out your different qualities, but also because girls move and girls change. Besides, too much togetherness can make twosomes tiresome. Can you enjoy your friends without closing yourself off to the rest of the class? Can you manage not to mind when your friends hang out with other girls or with each other? Can you remember that you and your friends like each other— you don't own each other?

I can't get it all from one friend.

36

Friendship is a plant that one must often water.

German proverb

Sometimes you'll want to talk about family, school, boys. A good friend will be there. Sometimes your friend will need to talk and it will be your turn to listen, no matter how busy you are. If you take care of your friendships, the best ones can last for years. If you dump your friends when you're swamped with schoolwork, or when a more popular person shows up, or when your crush asks you out, your friendships will be long gone when you are looking for company or comfort.

Without water, flowers dry up, and without attention, friendships fade. But just as too much water can kill plants, too much attention can drive friends away. Neither ignore nor smother friends. Like you, they need to feel appreciated. Like you, they need room to be themselves and to reach out to others.

Are you a generous friend? Ringo Starr sang, "I get by with a little help from my friends." His advice: "The ones you've got, take care of. Friends will save your life."

No one cares how much I know unless they know how much I care.

Never look down on anybody unless you're helping them up.

Jesse Jackson

$\mathcal{B}$e open-minded, not narrow-minded. Give the new girl in school a chance. Smile back to that friendly kid in chorus. Keep up with your best buddy from fourth grade even if the popular group dismisses her. And don't immediately assume that someone with a nose ring (or nose job) isn't worth getting to know.

Look to accept people instead of looking to reject them. Find what you like in someone, not what you dislike. A particular girl is not your cup of tea? Don't hang out with her. But must you whisper about her or tell her why she bugs you or mock her mannerisms? ("We are not amused," said England's Queen Victoria when she caught a staff member imitating her.)

According to Matthew in the Bible, Jesus said, "Judge not that ye be not judged." Next time classmates are being snide or mean about an acquaintance or friend, consider discouraging them. Say, "C'mon. Give her a break, or "He's not all that bad."

I will not make every day Judgment Day.

A show of envy is an insult to oneself.

Yevgeny Yevtushenko

Sure you wanted to win the school raffle. But what if your friend has the winning stub? Congratulate her. Later, when you win a contest or give a speech, she will cheer or root for you—rather than hope you mess up or seethe in secret.

Jealousy is natural. If your friend's room is jazzier than yours, you're bound to notice. But don't dwell on what she has; focus on what you have. Don't be competitive; work to feel proud of yourself. And know that even winners have troubles. No one really has it made. Satisfaction is never guaranteed.

What? You're green with envy because your neighbor's family got a new car? Get over it. According to the Bhagavad Gita, "Hell has three gates: lust, anger, and greed." Huh? You're plotting revenge because your ex–best friend hangs with your ex–second best friend? Move on already. Break free. "If you're going to hold someone down," Toni Morrison wrote, "you're going to have to hold on by the other end of the chain."

I will build myself up rather than put myself or my friends down.

39

I praise loudly; I blame softly.

Queen Catherine II

*F*lattery will get you nowhere? Ha! "Flattery'll get you anywhere," Jane Russell's character said in *Gentlemen Prefer Blondes*. Flattery is always welcome and is a great way to break the ice and make new friends.

When you don't know what to say to a girl, boy, or grown-up, pay a compliment like: "You draw so well" or "Cool scarf" or "Your field goal was incredible." Everyone likes to be praised, so why not praise in public?

How are you at accepting compliments? If someone says "I like your sweater," do you answer "This gross thing? I got it at the Salvation Army"? How does that make her feel? What if, instead, you just said "Thanks"?

You should be loud and lavish with praise, but if you criticize, keep it quiet and private. And think about this Jamaican saying: "When you point your finger at another person, look at where the other fingers point."

I will compliment at least one person every day.

Manners are a sensitive awareness of the feelings of others. If you have that awareness, you have good manners, no matter what fork you use.

Emily Post

Grown-ups are more apt to say "Why don't you invite Julia for dinner?" if Julia is big on pleases and thank-yous. But make no mistake; kids notice manners and social skills, too.

If you're saying hi to a bunch of friends, and Rachel walks over, instead of turning your back, open the circle and welcome her in. Say, "Hi. We were just talking about the gymnastics meet." Or, "You guys know Rachel, right?" What if you were about to mention that Michael— the guy who dumped Rachel—just asked out Emma? Have a heart. Save that tidbit for later.

Always consider other people's perspectives. Don't say "I'm glad I'm not an only child" if she is, or "My room is so small" if hers is half the size, or "Can't wait till the party" if she wasn't invited. Being polite is not a way to scam adults. It's a way to live.

Manners are not just for the dinner table.

*It was a delightful visit . . .
perfect in being much too short.*

Jane Austen

You've heard that guests and fish smell after three days? Sometimes it's even sooner.

Be a good guest—a friend, not a freeloader. Don't eat someone out of house and home. Don't appear at someone's door uninvited every afternoon. Don't phone because you're bored. "For what is your friend that you should seek him with hours to kill?" asked Kahlil Gibran. "Seek him always with hours to live."

Sleeping at a friend's? Try to leave before noon the next day. You and your friend will probably wake up tired, and so will her parents. Quit while you're ahead, and once you're home, don't race to the phone to catch up on your moments apart.

Joining a family for a weekend or holiday? Be helpful and polite and don't expect to be entertained every minute. Be willing and able when it's time to do dishes. Offer a present. Cookies you bake? Photos you take? And dash off a thank-you at the end of your stay. Warning: The longer you put off writing a thank-you note, the better it has to be.

I won't wear out my welcome.

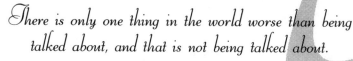

There is only one thing in the world worse than being talked about, and that is not being talked about.

Oscar Wilde

When you get up from the table in the lunchroom or get out of the car after soccer practice, you may hope that your left-behind friends don't say anything about you. And they may not. Chances are, your complexion or your poor grade or your mother's ugly shoes are a bigger deal in your mind than in theirs. You may wave farewell and they may go right on talking about birthdays or baby-sitting, movies or math tests.

But if the girls do discuss you, that's not so terrible. You talk about others, and others will talk about you. They might say something nice. Or someone might diss you while another defends you. Or someone may be jealous and express envy as contempt.

Being talked about is a small price to pay for being visible. Instead of hoping that everyone stays silent if your name comes up, hope that not too many people have to stop and ask, "Who's she?"

I don't like everybody.
Everybody doesn't have to like me.

43

Whoever gossips to you will gossip about you.

Lebanese proverb

*E*verybody gossips a little. As Barbara Walters said, "Show me someone who never gossips, and I'll show you someone who isn't interested in people." Gossip can bind friendships, clarify thoughts, and help you figure out where you fit in.

But gossiping can go too far, and some people can't resist badmouthing friends as well as strangers. Ben Franklin quipped, "To find out a girl's faults, praise her to her girlfriends." Is that true in your circle?

If you're laughing as one of your friends trashes another's clothes, handwriting, or taste in boys, know that when your back is turned she may open fire on you—or convert your big problem into her small talk. A girl who casually spreads rumors or breaches confidences is not to be trusted. So think before you bare your soul. And next time a person puts down someone you like, instead of laughing, defend her. At the very least, don't report back to the maligned friend. Don't relay hurtful insults in the name of higher truth. If you say, "Jessica told me she hates the way you dress," you're not being refreshingly candid. You're being as cruel as Jessica.

Those who engage in sharp-edged gossip often get cut.

44

Honesty is the best policy.

Aesop

esop's fables are wonderful to read and reread, and they teach a lot about right and wrong. But Aesop must have known that honesty is not *always* the best policy. You should strive to be honest with friends, parents, yourself. But use your judgment. Unless a situation is dangerous, tattling is rarely worth it.

A wise person knows when to say the truth instead of what someone hopes to hear and when to say what someone hopes to hear instead of the truth. In a store, for instance, it's okay to say, "I wouldn't buy those pants—they seem a bit snug." But if you're already in school when a girl asks, "Do these pants look okay?" the answer is simply "Yes."

Somerset Maugham wrote, "People ask you for criticism, but they only want praise." So be tactful. White lies have their place, and there's no need to start sentences with "No offense, but . . . "

I can be thoughtful as well as truthful.

*The day we see the truth and cease to speak is the
day we begin to die.*

Martin Luther King, Jr.

Truth is tricky. You probably wouldn't—and shouldn't—report an overheard insult or tell a friend that you can't stand her parents. But there are times when you must tell the truth, when disclosure beats discretion. If your best friend has a boyfriend, and you sometimes feel excluded, that's no reason to badmouth him. But what if she confesses that her boyfriend hits her? What if a close friend who is always dieting reveals that she hardly eats anything at all anymore? What if a friend who is often depressed says she's thinking of killing herself? What should you do?

Speak up! It may seem easier to stay mum, but is it easy to swallow your words day after day? And how would you feel if something terrible happened? Tell your friend you respect and love her and that you're worried about her. Confide in a trusted adult (parent, teacher, counselor, member of the clergy) to get her more help and information. In such cases, you're not betraying her confidence. You may be saving her life.

Good friends speak up. At least once.

Friendship is one eye closed, one eye opened.

Chinese proverb

*J*ust because you offer your friend good advice doesn't mean she's going to take it. You can tell her that cupcakes and cigarettes make a lousy lunch, but that doesn't mean she's going to sit down tomorrow with soup, salad, and milk. You can say that she's getting a reputation as a flirt, but that doesn't mean she'll change her ways by Wednesday. And you can confess that you don't see what she sees in her greaseball of a boyfriend but that doesn't mean she'll tell him he's history. (People's tastes and styles are different, and as Margaret Wolfe Hungerford put it, "Beauty is in the eye of the beholder.")

Despite your offer of sage advice, a friend may keep right on skipping lunch, skipping class, or worse. If her life or her health is in jeopardy, you can pipe up one more time or talk with your parent or a trusted adult. But if the situation is not dangerous, let matters go. It's her life, not yours. You may decide to become less close to her. Or you may decide that it's okay if you and a friend have different attitudes toward smoking, boys, school, everything.

I can choose my friends but I can't change them.

Avoid popularity if you would have peace.

Abraham Lincoln

Lots of girls yearn to be more popular. But who are the girls who really care about you? Do you have a friend you can call when you are excited—or upset? Do you have different friends who bring out your different interests? Do you feel free to be with whomever you want, boy or girl? If so, count yourself lucky.

Yes, the handful of popular kids are pleased that the masses have chosen to empower them. But some popular kids feel boxed in. Some feel pressured to act happy all the time. Some want to hang out with former friends, but they may be afraid to put their status at risk by being seen with girls who aren't "in," even though they may feel sad (and guilty) about letting grade school friendships slip away.

Does popularity have advantages? Sure. But it has disadvantages, too. As a Scottish proverb puts it: "A friend to all is a friend to none." Try not to dwell on one small knot of girls. Try not to obsess about individuals who aren't giving you a passing thought. Instead, show appreciation for your real friends and get to know girls who can become real friends.

A real friend is worth more than a fan club.

Reputation is an idle and most false imposition;
oft got without merit, and lost without deserving.

Shakespeare

How come your neighbor is in the cool group while there's a rumor going around about you? "Life," as David Letterman put it, "ain't all gum and root beer." And school can be particularly rough. Everyone knows everyone else's business. Everyone swims in the same puny fishbowl. And it's hard to change your reputation. But it can be done. (Rumors are short-lived—and you shouldn't believe all you hear, either!)

If you kowtow to popular kids, desperate to penetrate their inner circle, your standing and sense of self are going to go down the tubes. Says a Creole proverb: "Make yourself a floor mat and people will wipe their feet on you." But if you decide to shake up your image, others will eventually notice. Change friends by being nice to kids outside your clique. Sign up for after-school activities and branch out even if people think of you as 100 percent jock, brain, or artist. Dress in a new way that is more (or less) eye-catching. Become an expert at something. Bottom line: You're driving your bus, so if you're stuck in a ditch, rev your engines and climb out!

It's never too late to clean the slate.

Remember, no one can make you feel inferior without your consent.

Eleanor Roosevelt

Have you ever said, "He made me so mad" or "She makes me feel like a loser" or "The teacher made me feel stupid"? How can anyone really *make* you feel anything? They're *your* feelings. If a person you like acts aloof, that's disappointing. But why let her behavior toward you cast a shadow on your opinion of yourself? If certain people don't recognize your strengths, that's their loss. If your latest crush doesn't embrace you, he isn't rejecting you; he just isn't picking you out of the crowd.

How come that girl in homeroom is acting stuck up anyway? Is she insecure? Jealous? Is her home life hell? Did she not make captain or cheerleader? Did someone cut her down? Let her negative energy be her problem, not yours. Why feel the mood she wants you to feel?

Do not give other people power over you. Keep that power for yourself.

If they can't tell I'm amazing, they need new glasses.

The colander said to the needle,
"Get away, you have holes in you!"

Indian proverb

Why does a particular girl drive you bonkers? Is it because she, like you, wants to be an excellent student or phenomenal basketball player? Is she, like you, a little too concerned about how she measures up—physically and socially?

If someone bothers you, ask yourself why. It may have as much to do with you as it does with her. It's hard to watch someone strain to be popular or impress a teacher or attract a guy—if you know you've been there. Or perhaps she reminds you of your bossy sister, annoying cousin, or someone you can't write out of your life. Or perhaps she brings out your competitive side. You want to be the fastest, brightest, best. Fine. It's natural to feel that way. But can you strive to outdo yourself, not just others?

Whenever you and someone else have qualities or interests in common, try to make that a recipe for friendship instead of rivalry or animosity. As E. B. White wrote: "One of the most time-consuming things is to have an enemy."

When I don't like someone,
I can learn from it.

51

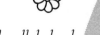

Help thyself, and God will help thee.

Jean de La Fontaine

When La Fontaine penned these words, he was not—repeat, not—referring to shoplifting. If you ever find yourself in a group of girls who are starting to steal, drink, vandalize, harass others, or do anything that makes you cringe, think about speaking up or moving on. Why risk your health or break a law? Why do something that makes you uncomfortable? Why go where you don't want to go?

"Oh, c'mon, just take the mascara. Who's going to know?" Answer: You. You'll know. And possibly a store guard. And the police. And your parents.

You don't have to report your friends if you don't want to. You don't have to say a word. But if you do say, "I don't want to steal [or drink or fight]," someone else in your group may admit she doesn't want to either. There is such a thing as positive peer pressure. There is also such a thing as making new friends. After all, by choosing to spend so much time with a certain girl or guy or group, you are choosing not to spend that time with other people —people who could become friends.

If it's risky or wrong, I won't go along.

52

Lily smiled at her classification of her friends. How different they had seemed to her a few hours ago! Then they had symbolized what she was gaining, now they stood for what she was giving up.

Edith Wharton

Are your friends changing? Or is it you? Some friendships that are quickly made, quickly fade. Other friendships that started long ago peter out. "My friends don't seem to be friends at all but people whose phone numbers I haven't lost," a character muses in a Nick Hornby novel. If, week after week, you don't like your friends as much as you'd like to, it may be time to drift apart.

Say your tomboy friend becomes boy crazy, your horseback riding pal spikes her hair, and you have gotten heavy into hockey. You are all out of sync. As Lillian Hellman said, "People change and forget to tell each other." You don't have to be mean as you step away, and you shouldn't ditch a loyal friend who is going through a stressful time. (Why bite the hand that needs you?) But if you do want to expand your social horizons, you can.

It's your friend who's getting restless? Give her a little room. And if she starts friend-hopping, you go friend-shopping.

I don't need friends who don't need me.

Waste not fresh tears over old griefs.

Euripides

You're slowly easing into a new clique—or at least bonding with a new girl. But you still miss your ex–best friend. It still hurts when you see her hanging with that other girl in the hall or at the mall. You still remember the fun times you two had together—at your home, at her grandmother's, at slumber parties, in swimming pools, on Halloween, on Rollerblades, in front of her television and your computer, and even when you went with her to get her ears pierced.

Of course you're sad! "When a lovely thing dies, smoke gets in your eyes." That's from a Jerome Kern song. He wasn't talking cigarettes, he was talking tears. Misting up.

The fact that you're still hurting shows that you have a big heart and that you really cared about your friend. Go ahead and soak your pillow. But then dry your eyes and focus on today and on new friends, girls and guys. Join a team or the band or an after-school group. Get involved. "Action," wrote Joan Baez, "is the antidote to despair."

When a friendship ends, I will grieve.
But not forever.

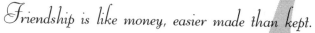

Friendship is like money, easier made than kept.

Samuel Butler

*F*riends move and friends change. But if you and another girl want to be close forever, there are ways to protect your friendship. And according to a Yiddish proverb, "One old friend is better than two new ones."

Can you stay in touch even during camp or vacation or if one of you moves? Can you telephone or exchange postcards, letters, or E-mail? Can you schedule visits? Keep the bridge intact. Don't get hung up on who owes whom a letter and how many pages it is. The point is to communicate, not to keep count.

If you and a friend have had a fight, can you find your way out of it? Were you displacing anger—were you actually mad at your gym teacher, not your friend? Even if that's not the case, try to work things out. Instead of saying, "Well, it was your fault!" try "Sorry I got mad." Or "I miss you and I want us to make up." Or "Come over; I bought rum raisin—your favorite." Or "Even Khaki the cocker spaniel has been wondering where you've been." Don't discard friendship. "It's easy to throw something into the river," goes a Kashmir saying, "but hard to take it out again."

Better to lose an argument than to lose a friend.

Love

One word frees us of all the weight and pain of life: That word is love.

Sophocles

You feel like singing! You feel like dancing! You feel like doing cartwheels and sliding down the banister and hugging your guinea pig! You look in the mirror and wink. Every lyric of every song on the radio is speaking to you. You can't wait to get to school, but as you dress, you daydream. You head to the bus stop, and the drizzle feels like sunshine. You marvel at the green of the trees and the scent of the air. You look at the flowers in your neighbor's garden and they seem gloriously, painfully, strikingly beautiful.

Could this be love?

Maybe. There's nothing as invigorating as love, especially when it's with a warm and wonderful person who loves you back. But take it slowly. One-way love can be frustrating, and you can drive yourself crazy over an impossible crush or spend years obsessing about someone who doesn't even know your name. Enjoy caring about a person, yes. But don't let love make you miserable.

Falling in love is fun; stepping in is wise.

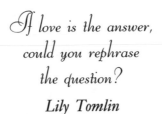

If love is the answer,
could you rephrase
the question?
Lily Tomlin

True or false: Everyone has a boyfriend except you. Though couples are very visible in school and at the pool or the park, most girls and guys have not paired off. Whether you have or haven't, what's important is to feel whole even when you are alone. You are not half a person waiting to be completed. You are a whole person with thoughts and feelings you may be ready to share.

Friedrich Nietzsche wrote, "One must learn to love oneself . . . with a wholesome and healthy love, so that one can bear to be with oneself and need not roam."

Love yourself and you seem friendly and likeable. Loathe yourself and you seem needy and desperate. Everyone feels lonely at times, but if you appreciate your own company and are able to enjoy reading a book or writing in a journal or taking a solitary walk, you'll be better off than if you depend on constant companionship.

I won't give all my love away;
I'll save some for myself.

Don't threaten me with love, baby.
Let's just go walking in the rain.

Billie Holiday

Some girls hurl themselves headfirst into love. Others take their time before signing on with one person.

More than one thousand years ago, Japanese poet Ono No Komachi wrote:

> *Though I go to him constantly*
> *on the paths of dream,*
> *never resting my feet,*
> *in the real world,*
> *it doesn't equal a simple glance.*

Are you yearning for a simple glance? Or are you content for now with having dreams and crushes rather than love?

Taking things slowly has its advantages. And as Jorge Luis Borges warned, "To fall in love is to create a religion that has a fallible god."

Having a boyfriend is not necessarily better than having a crush.

*If only one could tell true love from false love as
one can tell mushrooms from toadstools.*

Katherine Mansfield

One of your classmates won't stop talking about a
blue-eyed movie star. Another is hung up on the
lead guitarist of a British band. Another is head over heels
for the soccer coach or her best friend's boyfriend. Another is pumped about a boy she met at camp two summers ago even though he has ignored each of her
weekly letters. . . .

Though Cupid often misses his mark, some girls enjoy
one-way romances. But others do not enjoy pining over
passions that are out of reach, off-limits, or just plain
hopeless. While it's not always possible to control feelings,
most infatuations are like small flames. You can snuff them
out or fan them into a fire. If a lopsided or forbidden
romance is bumming you out, try to set yourself free.
Then stay on the lookout for available guys who are worth
your time and affection.

Changing crushes is not only permissible, it's instruc-
tive. "Falling out of love is very enlightening," wrote Iris
Murdoch. "For a short while you see the world with
new eyes."

*A boyfriend should not just be a love object.
A boyfriend should be a friend.*

And if I loved you Wednesday,
Well, what is that to you?
I do not love you Thursday—
So much is true.

Edna St. Vincent Millay

A new heartthrob every day may be a bit much, but you are entitled to change your mind about your feelings. You may like someone less as you get to know him more. Or you may give up on the crush who has never looked your way. Or you may find that it's the boy next door who puts a skip in your step.

That's fine. This is the time for learning what sort of people you are drawn to.

Guys can be fickle, too. A Shakespeare song goes: "Sigh no more, ladies, sigh no more, men were deceivers ever; one foot in sea and one on shore; to one thing constant never."

Romance does not come with guarantees, and at this stage it's probably just as well. After all, doesn't changing your mind make more sense than thinking about a guy who isn't thinking about you, or clinging to a guy you no longer really like?

Just because a boy and I like each other today doesn't mean we should get married tomorrow.

If you want to be loved, be lovable.

Ovid

What kind of guys do you fall for? Do they mumble and mope? Do they frown and scuff their feet and act colossally bored all the time? Probably not. Chances are they are energetic, good-looking, smart, and smiling. (Like you, right?)

If you're looking for romance, you could simply hang out in front of the mirror and nag your parents for new clothes. But why not stay busy and have fun as you find out what excites you and what you're good at? Theater? Sports? Politics? French? Science? Writing? Horses? Guitar? Cooking? Computer? Choir?

How many great guys have you met while watching the tube? It's while pursuing different activities that you are likely to meet someone interesting who is interested in pursuing you. And when you two do meet, will you be prickly, snobby? No way. As Arthur Guiterman wrote:

> *The porcupine, whom one must handle gloved,*
> *May be respected, but is never loved.*

Lovable? C'est moi.

I must endure the presence of two or three caterpillars if I wish to become acquainted with the butterflies.

Antoine de Saint-Exupéry

*E*ndure caterpillars to befriend butterflies? Kiss toads to find a prince? You may have a hard time even saying hello, never mind actually getting to know guys or going out on dates. Lots of people get timid and tongue-tied. But if you can talk to girls, you can talk to guys. Try to be friendly (not flirty) and approachable (not locked in an impenetrable clique).

No crush? No problem. You can still have boy buddies. Think of boys as boys. Not as status symbols or as members of the opposite sex.

What if someone you don't like likes you? Can you be nice without leading him on? He's got good taste, so why ridicule him? If he's not getting the message that his feelings aren't mutual, try ignoring him. Or if necessary, let him down gently. Tell him (privately) that you like him just as a friend or that you're not looking to go out with anyone.

At first romance may seem hit-or-miss. But you'll get better at figuring out whom you like and who will like you. It all starts with a hello and a smile.

I will not die from saying hi.

The act of longing for something will always be more intense than the requiting of it.

Gail Godwin

*J*ust say a girl has her eye on a guy. She notices what he wears to school, where he sits at lunch, whom he talks to in the halls. She knows when he leaves which class and which bus he takes home. She melts when he smiles and would give anything anything anything to go out with him.

Usually, nothing happens. He doesn't single her out. He dates some other girl. Her best friend; her worst enemy. But once every blue moon, the two become a couple.

Even then, things sometimes fizzle. Sure, many couples go the distance. But most students aren't meant to be each other's first and only love. Hard to believe, but a girl who has been fixated on someone for months may find that after the first exciting phone calls they have little to talk about. Or that their ideas and values are miles apart. Or perhaps they will go out for a month before she discovers that watching him fix his car or drum with his band isn't all that enthralling after all. As Candice Bergen once put it, "Dreams are, by definition, cursed with short life spans."

Some dreams, if realized, would be nightmares.

66

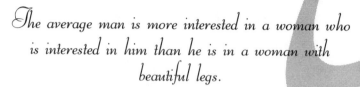

The average man is more interested in a woman who is interested in him than he is in a woman with beautiful legs.

Marlene Dietrich

Show-stopping legs can grab a guy's attention. But to keep his attention—or win his heart—there must be a meeting of the minds.

Boys notice cute girls, but they fall for girls who laugh at their jokes, ask them about their weekends, compliment their shirts or their haircuts, and tune in to what they have to say. They like girls who like them (and who like themselves).

It goes both ways. Have you noticed that boy with the biceps? Probably. More beguiling still is the boy who has noticed you. The one who smiles and who doesn't yawn or interrupt or walk away when you talk. The friendly one who pays attention to you.

If your heart is set on a boy who already has a huge fan club, he may not notice one more admirer. If, however, you discover someone on your own and show interest, sparks may fly.

Half of love is listening.

*The heart has its reasons
which reason knows nothing of.*

Blaise Pascal

The Chinese have a saying: "One dog barks because it sees something; a hundred dogs bark because they heard the first dog bark." Did someone in your school decide a particular guy was hot and now everybody has fallen for him? How about you? How does your taste in guys differ from your friends'?

If the football hero or the theater star drives others wild but casts no spell on you, more power to you. It's good to think and feel for yourself. Perhaps your heart is set on the quiet foreign exchange student who sits behind you in math. (Your friends don't get it.) Or on the class clown, whose grades don't come anywhere near yours. (Your parents don't get it.)

You can't always explain love—and you don't have to. You, not your peers or your parents, are the one with your feelings, and unless your guy is in jail or en route, you don't need to justify your attraction. Even to him. If you two have fun together, talking and laughing, you don't have to pick apart your relationship, constantly figuring out what is and isn't working and why. You can just relish your moments together.

I will not analyze everything to death.

The great question . . .
which I have not been able to answer despite
my thirty years of research into the feminine soul, is
"What does a woman want?"

Sigmund Freud

*D*ifferent women want different things. Most want a caring companion, a person who can accompany them to a concert or a movie, a person who can cheer them on at a field hockey match or a school play. Most look for a partner they like and respect and who likes and respects them.

In their rush to have a boyfriend, however, some girls are reckless with their hearts. They forget that the point isn't just to get a guy but to build a wonderful relationship with a wonderful guy. Some girls settle too soon for someone selfish or unworthy. He's happy to kiss her, but he doesn't care about her cares.

Can you hang on to your self-respect and your standards as you think about who intrigues you and why? Can you be thoughtful with your heart? "Love is a game two can play and both can win," said Eva Gabor.

I will not shortchange myself.

69

The human race, to which so many of my readers belong, has been playing at children's games from the beginning, and will probably do it till the end, which is a nuisance for the few people who grow up.

G. K. Chesterton

From Juliet to Jasmine, romance is complicated. Playing games or using go-betweens can make matters worse.

If you play hard to get, he may not be able to decode your scrambled signals. If you enlist a friend to test the waters, she may botch the job. What if she proclaims your undying love in front of the whole cafeteria? What if she jumbles up his heartfelt answer? What if she starts flirting with him herself?

Rather than play games, be direct. Don't *tell* him how you feel, *show* him. Don't put him on the spot with a point-blank "Do you like me?" Smile, talk, laugh, listen, compliment, ask questions, sit by him, look at him. And notice if he's smiling back and holding up his end of the conversation.

He is? Hurray! He's not? His loss. Accept this and move on. Who wants an unenthusiastic boyfriend anyway? And who wants a guy who doesn't know a gem (you!) when he sees one?

I will show, not tell.

Be not angry that you cannot make others as you wish them to be, since you cannot make yourself as you wish you to be.

Thomas à Kempis

Before you announce that your new boyfriend is the cutest, funniest, smartest, most talented person in the world, do a reality check. Is he perfect? Is anybody?

"Love involves a peculiar unfathomable combination of understanding and misunderstanding," wrote photographer Diane Arbus. The air between you is hypercharged. You sparkle extra for him and he sparkles extra for you. You get along so well and you want him to accept you completely, so—poof!—you decide he feels your every feeling, believes your every belief, and will be there forever. That's the magic of early love. Then one day he hurts your feelings or says something outrageous. Does this mean he's a lout and your love is a sham? Or could it just mean that your initial expectations were unrealistic?

I will try not to put others on pedestals.
It makes it too easy for them to fall off.

Nothing great is created suddenly,
any more than a bunch of grapes or a fig.
I answer you that there must be time.
Let it first blossom, then bear fruit, then ripen.

Epictetus

Are you in a hurry to have a boyfriend? Can you slow down and be discriminating? Make sure of your feelings and of his. Get to know each other in different moods, different months. Enjoy the phases of courtship. Don't rush to make affection official or to label it love or to exchange first kisses.

Kissing means more when feelings and trust have had time to grow. If you kiss a boy you just met, he may act like a stranger the next day—and he may be one. If you kiss a boy you've been going out with for a long time (three days is not a long time), it may be a memory you will cherish for the rest of your life.

"The remembrance of your love crept into my heart like spring quietly invading the wilderness . . ." wrote Faiz Ahmed Faiz, a Pakistani poet, "like the patient, who for no reason, suddenly has a sense of well-being."

I will wait until the time is right.

Love is like quicksilver in the hand.
Leave the fingers open and it stays.
Clutch it and it darts away.

Dorothy Parker

You like him. He likes you. Things are looking good. Should you meet him after every class? Announce that you're going out? Insist that he never smile at another girl?

Love, like a cat, resists being cornered. If you get possessive, he may want to bolt. And if you worry every time he talks to another girl, you may drive him and yourself crazy.

So what if he chats with other females? Isn't his dynamic enthusiasm one of the qualities you like about him? So what if you talk to other guys? Isn't your friendly openness one of the qualities he admires in you? Do you really want to dampen each other's spirits?

The best way to fight "the green-eyed monster" (as Shakespeare called jealousy) is to have faith not just in your boyfriend but in yourself.

Love is not a mousetrap.

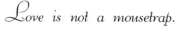

73

Say "I love you" to those you love.

George Eliot

If you have a boyfriend, let him know you appreciate him. The more graciously you love, the more you are loved. Instead of taking love for granted, can you celebrate it? Can you exchange little presents, compliments, notes, words? Can you reassure those you care about that you think of them often and fondly?

Be aware that "I love you" means different things to different people. "The word 'love' has by no means the same sense for both sexes, and this is one of the serious misunderstandings that divide them," wrote Simone de Beauvoir. There is no urgent need to say "I love you" to the boy you just started going out with. Wait longer and the words mean more. If it's really love, won't there be time for pronouncements? If it's not—if the relationship might be kaput by Friday—then all the more reason not to go on record with the *L* word.

Some boys say "I love you" too often. If he whispers he loves you even though you don't know each other well, try not to lose your bearings or feel pressured to repeat the words. You can tell him how much you care about him or how happy you are with him. But say "I love you" only if you mean it.

I will celebrate those I love.

Let there be spaces in your togetherness.

Kahlil Gibran

Why smother each other? Why stick together like superglue? Why press redial the moment you hang up? Give each other breathing room and you'll have more to talk about when you're hand in hand.

Pay attention to each other, yes, but keep doing what you did before he came along. See your girlfriends, do your homework, practice the trombone, surf the net. He, too, should stay involved with friends, schoolwork, extra-curricular activities. You want to be adding to each other's lives, not taking away. And you want to continue growing as individuals, not pressing pause on your development.

Rainer Maria Rilke wrote: "Love consists in this, that two solitudes protect and border and greet each other." Resist the urge to merge: One half plus one half equals only one. Be individuals: One plus one equals two.

My love life is not my whole life.

O fie miss, you must not kiss and tell.

William Congreve

When someone tells you a secret, you should not pass it on as though playing a game of telephone. Be a keeper of secrets and people will open up to you. Be a blabbermouth and no one will tell you anything worth blabbing.

And when it's your secret? Your cool crush? Your hot date? If you don't want anyone to know, don't tell anyone. If you truly want to discuss something, be candid with one trustworthy friend. There is no need to make your private life public or to post your boyfriend's love note on the Internet. If you do spill your news far and wide with a promise-not-to-tell tag line, your buddies may use your secret to spice up their conversations. It's too much to hope that they can keep their mouths closed if you cannot.

One way to avoid turning your life into the next school rumor is to confide in a friend or cousin in another town rather than in someone in your homeroom. Even so, proceed at your own risk. As the Talmud puts it: "Thy friend has a friend, and thy friend's friend has a friend; be discreet."

To kiss and tell is all very well,
but it's better to kiss and shut up.

We must develop and maintain the capacity to forgive. He who is devoid of the power to forgive is devoid of the power to love.

Martin Luther King, Jr.

Your boyfriend was an hour late, and you're mad. Yet he's usually prompt. And he did apologize profusely. And it wasn't entirely his fault. And he understands why you're angry.

What to do? Let him off the hook.

If you care about someone, is it worth it to stay mad or bear grudges? Rather than hold on to a hurt, express your disappointment, talk it over, and move on.

Love is not static. Once you have a boyfriend, it's not as though you put a big check mark by "Love" and that's that. Romances ebb and flow, wane and grow. As Ursula K. LeGuin wrote, "Love doesn't just sit there, like a stone. It has to be made, like bread, remade all the time, like new."

Love requires adjustments and fine tuning. If you're the one who caused him pain or did him wrong, don't be too proud to say you're sorry. Reconciliation can bring you closer than ever.

I will not simmer in silence.

He that cheats me once, shame on him;
he that cheats me twice, shame on me.

Scottish proverb

To err is human; to forgive, divine. But if you keep forgiving and forgiving and forgiving, he's a jerk and you're a chump.

Let's just say your steady boyfriend of several months kissed another girl while you were away on spring vacation. You would never have known except that her best friend told you. Now you're devastated. He confesses all, apologizes, and says he loves you and hopes you'll forgive him. Fine. You do. But what if you find out that he and she went on a date the next Saturday, even though he told you he was going bowling with the guys? Now what?

Cut your losses. Don't blame her; blame him. Do you want a steady boyfriend who can't be trusted? There are billions of guys in this world. He is just one. It's better to lose a boyfriend than to lose your dignity.

Just because love is blind doesn't mean I am.

No answer is also an answer.

German proverb

Whether you're at the start or at the end of a relationship, if your calls are not returned, your E-mail box is empty, your notes go unanswered, and he doesn't meet your eyes, take the hint.

Some boys are incapable of explaining why they feel the way they do. Some are too cowardly to tell you their ardor has cooled. And some count on your reading between the lines and knowing that a romance is over—or that it will never begin.

While gentle explanations might be handy, they are rarely offered. Many loves end abruptly or never get started, and no words ease the pain or clear the confusion.

What about when a boy likes you and you don't like him? Do you sit him down and tell him why? Or do you just go about your business and hope he gets the message? Silence is easy and can save face. That's why girls and guys both need to strive to figure out what others are saying, even when they aren't using words.

If the writing is on the wall, I will read it.

Hearts will never be practical
until they are made unbreakable.

L. Frank Baum

"Sometimes I wonder if men and women suit each other," Katharine Hepburn once mused. "Perhaps they should live next door and just visit now and then."

Not every romance is supposed to last forever, and not every great boyfriend would make a great husband or a great father. Still, it hurts when love turns to ash. When you open yourself to the joy of love, you also open yourself to the pain of loss. And some girls spend more time mourning than they do going out.

If you are newly alone, call your girlfriends—the ones you didn't drop the moment you had a boyfriend. Invite them over for a potluck dinner or an old-fashioned slumber party. Tell them how you're feeling and let them lift your spirits. Remind yourself and them how glad you are that they are there and how much they mean to you.

Though this particular boyfriend is now history, you'll meet someone else soon. Someone you may never have known had you been tied up in a relationship.

Girlfriends often last longer than boyfriends.

Love is so short and forgetting is so long.

Pablo Neruda

"'T is better to have loved and lost than never to have loved at all," said Alfred, Lord Tennyson. Be gentle with yourself. Don't bicycle past his home or play your song or cry for three days straight. Write a poem or get a new haircut or go to an art museum or catch up on your journal or organize your closet or read a mystery novel. Focus on friends, family, schoolwork, yourself. Get as busy as you were before that fateful first date.

Falling out of love can be harder than falling in. Don't deny the sadness—it is a tribute to your ability to love—but don't become the sadness either. If it helps you heal, remind yourself of the things that annoyed you about your ex . . . and the moments that weren't blissful.

You'll always remember your first love. Someday you'll even be able to recall the happy times with fondness instead of tears. You were important chapters in each other's lives. But there are many chapters still ahead. The end of one thing is the beginning of something else. And while memories are important, so is the here-and-now.

He was my first love—not my last love.

81

I have learned not to worry about love but to honor its coming with all my heart.

Alice Walker

With warm water and a day or two, you can force forsythia branches to burst into bloom. But you can't force someone to love you, and you can't love someone against your will.

So don't work so hard at it. Just continue to express yourself with honesty and humor, and keep encouraging those you care about to be open with you. Be friendly and allow others to confide in you about their worries and disappointments and hopes and ambitions. Allow them to be as real as you are.

When you least expect it, love will swing by again, in all its richness and complexity. As the Italians say, "Every hill has its valley." Lonely periods do end.

For now, can you maintain perspective? Did you lose your family in an earthquake? Do you have running water and food? How bleak are things really? "Learn to be happy," Pulitzer Prize-winning writer Anna Quindlen told graduates at a college commencement: Life can be "glorious, and you have no business taking it for granted."

Behind passing clouds, the sun still shines.

A lady of forty-seven who has been married twenty-seven years and has six children knows what love really is and once described it for me like this: "Love is what you've been through with somebody."

James Thurber

Many girls' mothers and fathers are no longer married. Many other girls listen to their parents argue and wonder, "Did they ever really love each other?" Chances are, they did—and still do. But adults suffer constant unromantic distractions, from paying bills and worrying about taxes to taking out the trash. Don't just roll your eyes at your parents' relationship. You may want to do things differently. But navigating the narrows together counts for something. And the day-to-day lifelong love married parents have is real, too—and in some ways harder to sustain than the love you and your friends enjoy on dates and at dances.

If your parents aren't together, you may feel extra-cautious about love (if you care about him, will he leave?). If your parents are constantly busy, whether they're married or divorced, you may feel extra hungry for love. No matter what your circumstance, try to find a balance of daring to love but protecting yourself, of being open but not being too vulnerable.

Family love counts, too.

Family

One of the oldest human needs is having someone to wonder where you are when you don't come home at night.

Margaret Mead

*N*ext time your mom or dad won't let you stay out late, ask yourself why they worry. Your parents look out for you because they love you. They're protective—possibly overprotective—out of concern for your safety.

You may think, "They don't trust me!" But is that really it? They may trust you but not the world. And, sad but true, they may have a point. The world isn't always trustworthy. Most strangers are nice; some are dangerous. Which is all the more reason why it's lucky to have a family. Parents who care. A door to close. A safe haven.

Families rule.

"I do think families are the most beautiful things in all the world!" burst out Jo, who was in an unusually uplifted frame of mind, just then.

Louisa May Alcott

Sometimes you may love your family as much as Jo loves hers in *Little Women*. Other times you may feel like George Burns, who said, "Happiness is having a large, loving, caring, close-knit family in another city."

When families get along, it's the best. Even when parents are too strict or busy or moody, it's good to know they're there. They can bail you out of a jam or pick you up if you get stranded far away. When you're sick, it's a parent, not a buddy, who helps in the middle of the night and serves up chicken soup the next day. And though siblings squabble, blood is thicker than water, and most siblings stick up for each other when necessary.

Do you treat your parents or siblings as though you're the sun and they're distant planets? Do they treat you the same way? What will happen if you treat them with respect and appreciation? It might set a better tone for everybody.

My family is not perfect, but neither am I.

*The joys of parents are secret,
and so are their griefs and fears.*

Francis Bacon

Even when your parents are testing you on spelling words or reminding your kid brother to flush the toilet, they have concerns of their own. They may be worried about bills, jobs, termites, health, their marriage, or their own parents.

If you want to be heard, it helps to listen. Can you ask your parents about their day at home or at work? When your parent comes home from a business trip, can you ask "How'd it go?" instead of "What did you bring me?" Think about what (besides you) might be on your father's mind right now and show interest or support. If your mother seems particularly preoccupied, consider saying "I miss you" rather than "You're always busy." That will warm her up rather than put her on the defensive. The trick is to find a balance between being a caring daughter and a daring person. Said novelist Amy Tan, "I made a promise to myself: I would always remember my parents' wishes, but I would never forget myself."

*I know where I come from,
and I'm finding out where I want to go.*

The greatest love is a mother's; then comes a dog's; then a sweetheart's.

Polish proverb

Sweethearts come and go. Moms stick around. Pearl S. Buck wrote, "Some are kissing mothers and some are scolding mothers, but it is love just the same, and most mothers kiss and scold together."

It's true that most mothers want your dress to cover your thighs. And for you not to dye your hair green. Or pierce your navel. Or get a tattoo. But just as you'd like to get along with your mom, she'd like to get along with you. Which means you have the same goal. Can you work on it? Can you find a moment between breakfast chaos and bedtime scramble to talk about what's new or has made either of you proud—or upset? If you've had a fight, can you make up? Use "I" not "You" sentences: "I disagree" not "You're wrong," or "I need some privacy" not "You're always butting in." Can you compliment your mom on her blouse, stew, accomplishment? Can you leave a note under her pillow or a message on her answering machine? If you behave toward her, for one minute, as warmly as you do toward your best friend's mom, you'll both come out ahead.

Nobody's mother gets it right all the time.

The mother-child relationship is paradoxical and, in a sense, tragic. It requires the most intense love on the mother's side, yet this very love must help the child to grow away from the mother and to become fully independent.

Erich Fromm

*P*arents try to give kids roots and wings.

Are you and your mom incredibly close? So close, in fact, that you don't want to go to slumber parties, try sleepaway camp, or fly to your aunt's in Florida for four days? Uh-oh. If you're too dependent on Mom, it may be time to walk out of her shadow and do more alone or with peers.

Are you at odds with your mother? Yesterday you loved it when she bought you dresses and held your hand while crossing streets. Today you hate whatever she brings home and you'd never hold her hand. Uh-oh. If you're forging your own identity so effectively that you're leaving Mom in the dust, please remember that she probably is not evil incarnate and that you can separate without disconnecting altogether.

My mother loves me in her way.

91

When I was a boy of fourteen, my father was so ignorant I could hardly stand to have the old man around. But when I got to be twenty-one, I was astonished at how much the old man had learned

in seven years.

Mark Twain

Are you mad at your dad? Did you announce that you were going to take a spin on Spike's motorcycle—and Dad blew a gasket? What is he? A tyrant? No. A dad. And chances are your father is not out to make your life miserable. Chances are he believes in you and wants you to be your best.

Hillary Rodham Clinton said, "My parents set really high expectations for me and were rarely satisfied. I would come home from school with a good grade and my father would say, 'It must have been an easy assignment.'" Infuriating? Yes. But he meant to be motivating—and perhaps he was.

Is your dad too tough? Does he, like you, sometimes fly off the handle? Is he too committed to his work? Or to a stepfamily? Years down the road, you may reassess your old man. You may even decide that he meant well and did what he could. Or just about. As Goethe wrote, "Life teaches us to be less severe with ourselves and others."

Growing up includes growing pains.

Nothing is dearer to an old father than a daughter.

Euripides

If you and your dad love each other, you're both blessed. If you and your dad can talk and laugh and play cards and run errands and see movies and share pistachio nuts, you are both extraordinarily lucky. Go wild. Leave him a note in his briefcase or jacket pocket. Or add zing to his voice mail or E-mail. Or just give him an extra smile and hug. And know that he, too, revels in your closeness and is proud of who you are. Not just your class election or good grades or goal in soccer or role in the play, but who you are. That's why some parents (male and female) call their child their "pride and joy." And that's why Christopher Morley said, "We've had bad luck with our kids—they've all grown up."

In the speech President Bill Clinton gave at his daughter Chelsea's high school graduation in 1997, he said, "I ask you . . . to indulge your folks if we seem a little sad or we act a little weird . . . a part of us longs to hold you once more as we did when you could barely walk, and to read to you just one more time *Good Night Moon*."

If I love my parent, I can say so.

93

An angry father is most cruel toward himself.

Publilius Syrus

What if your father is not too good to be true? What if he's not a Nick-at-Nite kind of dad? One of your friends may have a devoted father. What if yours is grumpy or absent or drunk?

That's harsh. Many kids have complicated home lives. But that doesn't make yours any easier.

"It is impossible to please all the world and one's father," wrote Jean de La Fontaine. If your father is always disapproving and refuses to get professional help, there may come a point where you will need to stop looking to him for approval. If you continue to seek reassurance from a distant or abusive parent who just can't give it, you'll only feel worse. Better to try to accept his shortcomings and look elsewhere for guidance and support. Yes, this is a shame for you and a loss for your parent. While he's yelling (or just plain gone), he's shutting himself off from a bond that could have been wonderful for both of you. But others may take a fatherly interest in you. And someday if you have kids of your own, you can be there for them. Who knows? In the future, you and your parent may even accept (and forgive) each other and may manage an adult-to-adult relationship after all.

I can bloom even in thin soil.

Much unhappiness has come into the world because of bewilderment and things left unsaid.

Fyodor Dostoyevsky

You think your mom has been acting weird or mean or distracted because of your school conference. But it's really because she's worried about layoffs at work. She thinks you've been acting sullen because you're mad at her. But actually you're mad at your best friend for flirting with your boyfriend.

Can you try harder to fill in the blanks for each other? If your parents are trying to talk about something that makes you uncomfortable, make an effort to hear them out. And if you want to broach an awkward subject, try to do so over dishes or in a car or on the phone. Heart-to-hearts are sometimes easier when you're not face-to-face.

Some girls complain that their parents invade their privacy. No one should read your diary or listen in on your calls. But don't be so secretive that you leave your parents in the dark. If they ask "Where are you going?" and you mumble "Out," that won't lead to deeper trust or closer communication. And parents do need to know what you're up to.

I won't shut out my parents.

*Parents are not quite interested in justice,
they are interested in quiet.*

Bill Cosby

Some parents struggle to help their children resolve conflicts; some accidentally pit their kids against one another; and some just wish their children would work things out on their own.

If your parents have given you negotiating skills and a healthy respect for one another, you're ahead of the game. If, instead, they label you ("the pretty one," "the brain," "the little one") or prod you to compete ("On your mark, get set, go! Winner gets a treat!"), that's less ideal.

Try to think of your siblings as teammates, not rivals. You will be important to each other all your lives, so you might as well make peace—for your sake and your parents'. Can you praise each other instead of cut each other down? Can you seek different activities and ways to shine instead of signing up together for ballet, band, or baseball? Experiment, for three minutes, by treating your siblings with the same courtesy you reserve for friends then seeing how they respond. You can't break up with your family, but you can break old patterns.

I can call the truce.

Cruel is the strife of brothers.

Aristotle

Raise your hand if you adore your brother. Now raise both hands and hug him.

Too many families are rife with fraternal friction. If you and your brother constantly snarl, snap, bite, and fight, remind yourself that you are not lion cubs picking over a dead wildebeest. You're humans. You can do better.

Next time your brother taunts you, don't tell on him— talk to him. Say you're sorry you two don't get along better. Compliment something, anything. ("Your room looks neat." "You're so good at———.") Instead of bickering, offer popcorn or homework help, or ask his advice, or talk about a relative. Get a decent relationship going— it's not impossible. As Mother Teresa said, "Kind words can be short and easy to speak, but their echoes are truly endless."

If you are the one who picks fights, try to change your ways. If he starts them, say, "I don't want to argue." And if you always ban your kid brother from your room, invite him in for a quick game of cards or Clue or Sorry. It may make his day.

When brothers and sisters fight, nobody wins.

Big sisters are the crabgrass in the lawn of life.

Charles Schulz

Some sisters get along famously. Others fight like cats. The most fortunate sisters are those who become friends for life.

Are you in the shadow of a super sister? Work on your own strong suits. Does your big sister boss you around? Stick up for yourself without shouting or pouting. Do you have a crush on her boyfriend? Don't even think about acting on it. Is your sister away at camp or school? Write or send a care package.

Are you the big sister? You can be teacher, friend, ally. Encourage your kid sister, in school and out. Ask how a test or audition went. Do chores or errands together. Recognize that she has some strengths you don't. And share—you'll both reap benefits. (If you tease her about being a nerd instead, she may get nerdier—and hate you, too.)

Will you two get along every minute? No way. But as Mahatma Gandhi said, "It is possible to live in peace." Learning how to befriend, not belittle, siblings also teaches you to compromise, cooperate, and be comfortable with people outside your family.

I can be civil to my siblings.

*Those whom we can love, we can hate;
to others we are indifferent.*

Henry David Thoreau

*J*ust as a quarrel between parents can sometimes get loud, you and your sibling may sometimes get into a doozy of a fight: "I wish you were never born!" "I hate your guts!" "You are such an idiot!" "You are the stupidest person in the world."

You get this mad because you love each other. You'd never shriek at someone you just met. You'd never say you hate the school nurse. But when you really care about someone, and you feel safe enough to express your rage, fights can get fierce. Why? Because deep down you believe that your relationship can survive.

Accept the range of emotion that is part of family life. Anger, like a summer thunderstorm, comes and goes. But temper your temper. Don't fire the first shot or insist on firing the last. Strive to follow the advice of Will Rogers: "Live so that you wouldn't be ashamed to sell the family parrot to the town gossip."

When people care, passions flare.

There is no such thing as fun for the whole family.
Jerry Seinfeld

This is almost true, especially if your family includes both toddlers and teens. But instead of slamming your bedroom door, blasting your music, and being mad that your family never does fun things together, think about how you (yes, you) can come up with a creative solution.

The whole family might enjoy renting a classic movie, like *The Wizard of Oz.* Or going out for pizza or ice cream or a walk. Or making bread or soup or sugar cookies. Or playing hearts or charades or Monopoly. Or spending a day at a beach, lake, or mountain. (No squabbling, and you may get to go again.)

Start your own traditions. Saturday evening banana splits. Sunday morning pancakes. A weekly letter to Grandmom—everyone writes a paragraph. A once-a-week after-dinner reading—everyone reads a poem or a passage from a book aloud. Different ages, different choices, but no teasing, because the point is family closeness.

With a good plan and a good attitude, I can help make a day memorable.

Remember that as a teenager you are at the last stage in your life when you will be happy to hear that the phone is for you.

Fran Lebowitz

Want to reach out and touch someone? Some families fall apart because of the phone. Everyone wants to hog it. Or messages get mangled. Or no one respects call waiting and crucial calls never get through.

Set ground rules. During that rare event known as Family Dinner, it's a shame if Dad's on the horn to the office and you're discussing homework with a neighbor. Why not agree to screen calls during meals? (If the phone rings, it's probably not your heartthrob, but some stranger asking for a donation.) You can also discuss time limits (no calls after ten?) and limits on time (fifteen minutes?). And maybe your parents can invest in a separate line for the kids, an answering machine, or E-mail.

By the way, when you are on the phone, must you interrupt or yak endlessly? As Fran Lebowitz quipped, "The opposite of talking isn't listening. The opposite of talking is waiting." It's okay to be chatty. But if the person called you, find out why.

I will play fair with the phone.

Divorce is probably of nearly the same date as marriage. I believe, however, that marriage is some weeks the more ancient.

Voltaire

Many siblings fight one moment and are friends the next. Many parents argue, then make up. Yet for some parents, there is no reconciliation.

If your parents are divorced, the adjustment is painful and sad and slow. Who else in your class has parents who are divorced? In America, nearly one out of three kids lives with a single parent. Don't bottle up feelings. Talk with friends about denial, anger, guilt, hurt, shock, relief. If you keep wishing your parents would reconnect, be realistic and briefly remember the worst fights. Remind yourself, too, that the divorce was not your fault: Your parents divorced each other—not you. And as Margaret Trudeau said, "It takes two to destroy a marriage."

Try to appreciate both your parents, rather than take sides. If one parent gets you through homework and the other provides fun, fun, fun, both are trying to care for you. If one parent shuttles you from orthodontist to piano lesson, and the other sends gifts or cards, both are showing love. And if only one parent is there for you, that hurts, but the love of one parent can see you through.

I still have a family.

There are fathers who do not love their children; there is no grandfather who does not adore his grandson.

Victor Hugo

While some grandparents are more involved than others, most show off your photos, are eager for your news, and can't wait until your visits. Are your grandparents alive and well? Do you take them for granted?

Call, fax, and write letters. Send drawings, photos, E-mail, good report cards. Consider confiding. Grandparents have seen a lot and may have good advice. Many also have good stories—about the olden days and your own parent's misdeeds and exploits. What were your grandparents like at your age? What was your parent like as a kid? Ask.

Do your grandparents give you birthday or holiday presents? Do you blow off writing them thank-you notes? How would you feel if you sent someone a gift and never even heard if it got there? As for gift giving, sure, you can just sign your name on your parents' gift card. But why not make something yourself? Homemade stuff goes over big—whether it's edible, wearable, or ideal for displaying on the refrigerator or coffee table.

I will appreciate my grandparents.

103

If you wish to succeed, consult three old people.

Chinese proverb

Some kids and teenagers dismiss their wrinkled relatives as a bunch of old fogies. Mistake. Older people have been around for decades and will share stories and insights free of charge. Wisdom doesn't automatically come with age, yet many experienced adults are able to see situations clearly.

When your aunt or great-aunt offers advice on what to do about your teacher or boyfriend or neighbor, you don't have to heed it. But it doesn't hurt to hear her opinion.

Above all, don't act like you've been-there-done-that. Writer Mavis Gallant described a respectful man who "never once remarked, 'I've heard this before,' or uttered the timeless, frantic snub of the young, 'I know, I know, *I know.*'" Why not go ahead and show respect? Your older relatives will be flattered by the attention—even if you ultimately choose to take their advice with heaps of salt.

Aunts and uncles are there when I need them.

What is there to do when people die—people so dear and rare—but bring them back by remembering?

May Sarton

When a member of your family dies, you may feel that a part of you has died, too. Be gentle with yourself. Don't expect to feel better in a hurry. But don't deny yourself the right to ever laugh or feel good again. Share your sorrow with parents and siblings who may also be grieving. And, if possible, remember the loved one on paper: in a poem or sketch or melody or work of art.

Your relationship is safe now, and someday, in months or years, you'll be able to remember the good times with fondness instead of tears. You may also become stronger and more compassionate than you ever were before. You won't moan, "This is the worst day of my life" when you misplace your homework. You'll be able to distinguish little troubles from big ones. And you'll be able to comfort others in their moments of need.

A person who is dead can be alive and safe in my memory.

The sorrow for the dead is the only sorrow from which we refuse to be divorced. Every other wound we seek to heal, every other affliction to forget; but this wound we consider it a duty to keep open; this affliction we cherish and brood over in solitude.

Washington Irving

Of course we do. That's how much we loved the person who is gone, whether he or she is absent because of death or divorce. Death and divorce are extremely hard to accept. But as architect Maya Lin said, "Only when you accept the pain can you come away from it."

If months and months go by and you don't feel one bit better, give yourself permission to start bouncing back. It is not a betrayal of a dead or absent father to laugh or to smile at a mother's boyfriend. It is not a betrayal of a missing mom to joke and be silly with friends or to befriend your father's girlfriend.

No one would want you to grieve forever. Talk to a doctor or counselor if you find yourself tangled up in memories or anger. Then, without rushing things, invite yourself to enjoy life again.

I can be like a trick birthday candle: I can keep making a comeback.

106

Honor thy father and thy mother.

Exodus 20:12

Of course you should heed this commandment as well as the ones about, say, killing, stealing, and coveting. It makes sense to honor your parents. But some kids don't live with their parents. Some have parents who aren't honorable. And some never knew their birth parents but love and honor the adoptive parents who chose to love and raise them.

An African proverb says, "It takes a village to raise a child." Gloria Steinem once wrote: "The biological family isn't the only important unit in society; we have needs and longings that our families cannot meet."

If your parent or parents can't always be there for you, reach out to other trusted adults. You may find a mentor or role model in your aunt, teacher, coach, minister, priest, or rabbi. If you're an only child, enjoy the fact that your room is quiet, but look to cousins, neighbors, and friends. Find people who care about you and who matter to you—family or not.

Sharing love can be as important as sharing genes.

107

The great pleasure of a dog is that you may make a fool of yourself with him and not only will he not scold you, he will make a fool of himself too.

Samuel Butler

As Charles Schulz put it, "Happiness is a warm puppy." Dogs are family members, too. So are cats. And bunnies, guinea pigs, turtles, snakes, fish, frogs, hamsters, gerbils, mice, rats, iguanas, lizards, and birds of all sorts—even horses, if you're lucky. What am I overlooking here? A treasured ant farm? Beetles in a bug box? A pot-bellied pig? A cow?

After enduring much criticism, President Harry Truman once remarked, "If you want a friend in Washington, get a dog." Dogs and other pets are faithful when others let you down. They love you even on bad days and even when you want to be alone—but not totally alone.

Are you taking good care of your pet? Do you feed it on schedule? Keep its home clean? Show it affection? You can let your parents do all the work. But why not take on the job yourself? Tail wagging and purring will be your rewards. And you'll find satisfaction in feeling needed and doing an important job well.

My pet and I are lucky to have each other.

School

*Education is not the filling of a pail,
but the lighting of a fire.*

William Butler Yeats

School isn't just about making the grade and getting the diploma. It's about learning to learn and learning to love learning. About liking the novel you read in English so much that you search for another book by the same author. About enjoying Spanish class so much that you attempt conversation with someone who speaks only Spanish. About relishing how good it feels to solve a hard math problem. About botching the experiment in science, doing it over, getting it right, and realizing that failure can lead to success. About finding friends who make you laugh and friends who make you think. School can teach you how to keep your brain awake between classes, too. To observe, read, think, grow, learn. School can teach you to be a student of the world.

"Anyone who stops learning is old, whether at twenty or eighty," said Henry Ford. "Anyone who keeps learning stays young."

Others may sleepwalk, but I am awake.

The greatness of the human personality begins at the hour of birth. From this almost mystic affirmation there comes what may seem a strange conclusion: that education must start from birth.

Maria Montessori

When you were a suckling infant, a wide-eyed baby, a reckless toddler, and an adventuresome kindergartner, you were learning, learning, learning. Using your brain and five senses, you were processing information faster than a computer. And you still are. As Carl Sandburg pointed out, "Time is a great teacher."

By now you know more than where milk comes from and why ambulances have sirens and why you shouldn't pet a strange dog without asking its owner. You have knowledge. You have experience.

But you're not done. Keep asking questions—even if your parents can't answer them. Keep seeking answers—even if you have to consult several encyclopedias or visit various web sites. Keep your eyes and ears and mind open—even when you're walking down the same path or listening to the same teacher or dining with the same relative. If you approach the familiar in a fresh way, you'll keep learning. About the world and yourself. In school and out.

I can learn about many things and become an expert at something.

112

Men are taught to apologize for their weaknesses, women for their strengths.

Lois Wyse

Run with your talents. Live up to your potential. Be proud of your gifts. You're a great student? Raise your hand. Your butterfly stroke is awesome? Go for the gold. You draw lifelike portraits? Keep a sketch pad in your backpack.

If your prowess ever intimidates others, whose problem is that? This doesn't mean you should act superior. Just be superior. But also be considerate and confident and a good sport, not a competitive win-or-whine know-it-all. Then, if you happen also to be smart/athletic/artistic/stunning, try to enjoy the cards you were dealt and let others enjoy them, too. Friends won't be put off by your strengths unless you start getting an attitude or acting falsely modest. Which you won't, right?

You're worried a certain guy won't like you if you're better at tennis or math than he is? Excuse me? He'd prefer a klutz or a ditz? Let him find one instead of slowing you down. Strive to be your best and do your best, and you will attract guys who are inspired by excellence—not afraid of it.

I will never play dumb.

113

Ideas come from everywhere.

Alfred Hitchcock

The teacher says, "Write a poem." You think, "I don't know what to write."

Think again.

Write about the way shadows stretch. The way jeans fade. The way geese fly. The way you-know-who smiles. Write about Australia or Queen Elizabeth or M. E. Kerr. Write about Buddha or Bach or the Beatles. Write about *The Little Prince* or *The Great Gatsby*. Write about your favorite quote in this book.

Do you say "I don't know" when you could say "Let me think"? If you don't know a lesson, why not reread it? If you don't know why a friend is acting weird, why not replay your last conversation—putting yourself in her place? Don't say "I can't explain it" or "I don't get it." Try to explain it. Try to get it. Seek help early on. You can break through the fog and find the light.

I keep getting smarter.

The thousand-mile journey starts with one step.

Japanese proverb

Sometimes a teacher asks for a term paper, and the task starts to loom larger and larger in your mind until it seems all but impossible. You feel defeated, panicked, unable to begin.

What to do?

Begin. Stop thinking of it as scaling Mount Everest. Think of it as going for a walk, uphill perhaps, and take it step by step. Books like this begin with single quotes. Reports like yours begin with taking notes. Break your work into manageable chunks, push up your sleeves, and dig in, bit by bit by bit.

Even presidents and kings have to chip away at huge projects before feeling the satisfaction of completion. Said Calvin Coolidge: "We cannot do everything at once, but we can do something at once." Said England's Albert I: "The first reward of a work accomplished is having done it."

I won't get overwhelmed; I'll get started.

*Procrastination is the art
of keeping up with yesterday.*

Don Marquis

It's smart to work methodically and to accomplish your goals in a slow-and-steady way instead of a stop-and-start way. After all, what if something trips you up? Something bad, like falling on your chin and needing stitches? Or even something good, like being invited by your crush to a concert on Thursday when your report is due on Friday?

The work is not going to go away, so get it out of the way. Factor in a little margin and get the job done. Mark Twain quipped, "Never put off until tomorrow what you can put off till the day after tomorrow." But Benjamin Franklin said it straight: "One today is worth two tomorrows."

Once you start, it's easier to keep going. So stay organized. Keep lists of top-priority projects and daily assignments. Clear away clutter. Imagine how good it will feel when you finish.

If I don't fall behind, I'll come out ahead.

I arise in the morning torn between a desire to improve (or save) the world and a desire to enjoy (or savor) the world. This makes it hard to plan the day.

E. B. White

Do you plan your day? Are you aware of how you spend your time? "An inch of gold cannot purchase an inch of time," goes a Chinese saying.

Some people fritter away their days and fail to get their work done. Others stick to a ruthless schedule and forget to have any fun. It's a challenge to meet goals and to meet friends, to work and to work out, to get enough rest and to sleep. But you can decide what to do with your time.

Many people say "I don't have time to exercise" or "I don't have time to read for pleasure" or "I don't have time to practice piano." Yet everyone's day has the same twenty-four hours. Nobody gets more; nobody gets fewer. If something is important to you, don't wait until you have the time. Find the time. Make the time.

I won't take chances; I'll make choices.

The difference between the right word and the almost right word is the difference between lightning and the lightning bug.

Mark Twain

"So how's school?" asks your favorite aunt. "Fine," you say, adding, "My friends are nice and we're studying lots of interesting things." That's a whole lot better than grunting, but what have you really told your aunt? Not much.

Yes, a friend is nice. But is she also funny or graceful or shy or bilingual or generous or anxious or jealous or horse crazy or boy crazy? Yes, your class is interesting. But why not say you cried when you finished *Of Mice and Men*? Or that you learned why port cities like New York and New Orleans developed faster than inland cities. Give others something to talk to you about. Speak (and write) with precision. Search for the right word—*le môt juste*—instead of peppering your sentences with "you know" or "like" or lazy words or curse words. The more articulate and specific and eloquent you are, the more people will want to hear what you have to say. And the more succinctly you can speak, the better. "Brevity is the soul of wit," as Shakespeare's Polonius put it—after rambling on and on.

*I won't strain for big words.
I will strive to say what I mean.*

118

The struggle is what teaches you.

Sue Grafton

It's fun to be good at something. To be a whiz at math, a natural at science, the first one picked in gym.

Coasting along and doing what comes easily is fine. But if you never screw up, you may not be challenging yourself. Have you ever really put time and effort into a painting or a speech or a project or a sport? Have you ever stuck with something until you succeeded—and felt proud? Confidence and expertise come after practice and patience.

You may feel you have reached a plateau. You're okay at swimming but you'll never be great. You're proficient at French but you'll never be fluent. Can you keep going? Immerse yourself in the water—or the subjunctive. Find a coach or a teacher who can challenge and advise you. If you don't give up, you can reach your goals. As Euclid said, "There is no royal road to geometry." And as Samuel Johnson wrote, "What we hope ever to do with ease, we must first do with diligence."

Opening night comes only after days of rehearsal.

*Have you learned lessons only of those
who admired you, and were tender with you,
and stood aside for you? Have you not learned
great lessons from those who reject you . . .
and dispute the passage with you?*

Walt Whitman

Sooner or later everyone gets a teacher she does not like—or who seems not to like her. Last year's teacher would have given you an A. This year's teacher tells you to work harder. You probably badmouth her under your breath. But you may also stretch for a higher level of achievement. You may earn that A—and learn a lot in the process.

Of course, this year's tough teacher may not be a stimulating fireball but a drone who doesn't recognize a good student when she's staring at one. This happens. In real life as well, there are tiresome landlords, unfair employers, drippy colleagues. If what you wind up learning from a tough teacher isn't how to study harder, but how to make the best of a less than ideal situation, that too is educational. Besides, as Anna Freud put it, "Creative minds have always been known to survive any kind of bad training."

*If I want to make waves,
I can't always expect smooth sailing.*

They teach in academics far too many things and far too much that is useless.

Goethe

It can certainly feel that way. But you don't always know at age twelve or sixteen what you'll find useful (or essential) at age twenty or sixty. Today you may think, "Who cares about the conditional tense in French?" Then—voilà!—as an adult you might get transferred to Paris. Some lessons simply teach you to think, to question. Miguel de Unamuno wrote, "True science teaches, above all, to doubt and be ignorant."

School also exposes you to what's out there. T. S. Eliot wrote, "It is part of education to interest ourselves in subjects for which we have no aptitude." It's worth it to become a well-rounded person who can hold her own in any conversation and who can make a living in a satisfying way.

Euripides wrote, "Do not consider painful what is good for you." Reaction 1: Yeah, yeah, yeah. Reaction 2: Maybe he has a point.

I can get something out of anything.

121

My alma mater was books. . . . I could spend the rest of my life reading, just satisfying my curiosity.

Malcolm X

The reading of all good books is like conversation with the finest minds of past centuries.

René Descartes

A book is like a garden carried in the pocket.

Chinese proverb

One of the greatest pleasures in my life is to be reading a really good book . . . and to know that after that one will be another really, really good book, and another . . . and another.

Oprah Winfrey

I have never known any distress that an hour of reading did not relieve.

Montesquieu

Books are . . . funny little portable pieces of thought.
Susan Sontag

A book must be an ice ax to break the frozen sea within us.
Franz Kafka

Book, books, books. It was not that I read so much. I read and read the same ones. But all of them were necessary to me. Their presence, their smell, the letters of their titles, and the texture of their leather bindings.
Colette

.

Read in order to live.
Gustave Flaubert

Books are friends. (Thanks for having this one in your hands.)

It's never too late—in fiction or in life—to revise.

Nancy Thayer

You can rewrite and revise your life. And you can rewrite and revise your writing. Next time you finish a composition or an essay, congratulate yourself for having done the hard part but don't rush to hand it in. Before bed, or perhaps the next day or week, reread your work and make it even better.

Cross out repetitive words or sentences. Delete awkward phrases or stilted words like *thus* or *hence*. Check the spelling of words you aren't sure of. Give the ending more oomph. Read your work aloud to see if it's clear and to the point.

Most writers are rewriters. Said Vladimir Nabokov: "I have rewritten—often several times—every word I have ever published. My pencils outlast their erasers." Even if your words are not meant for publication, they are meant to be read. If you plan to sign your name to a report—or a love letter or a thank-you note—have enough self-respect to edit and proofread your work. And if you need to start something over, do so. "The wastepaper basket is a writer's best friend," said Isaac Bashevis Singer, a Nobel laureate.

I will reread my words before they leave my desk.

124

Every child is an artist. The problem is how to remain an artist once he grows up.

Pablo Picasso

If you love to draw or paint or dance or act or write poetry or do ceramics or take photographs, you don't have to stop just because you're out of grade school. Your teachers may no longer expect illustrated book reports, but that doesn't mean you can't keep sketching on your own or spending Saturdays at museums and galleries. Nurture the artist within yourself. It's hard to make a living as a dancer, but if you can't live without dance, why not give it a try—or at least continue attending classes and going to dance performances?

Why abandon artistic pursuits and pleasures just because you're devoting time to other subjects? Your aesthetic talents and appreciation can be useful in many fields (book design, graphic art, landscaping, interior decorating). Even your room and future office will probably always have a certain flair.

Being efficient counts, but so does being expressive. Work well, but dream, too. Albert Einstein wrote, "Imagination is more important than knowledge." The byway can lead to places the highway does not.

I will take care of the artist and the dreamer inside me.

Everyone has a talent. What is rare is the courage to follow the talent to the dark places where it leads.

Erica Jong

*A*rt requires bravery and commitment. Artists sometimes need to be selfish, yet it's generous to share your gift and your vision.

Maybe the dark place where your talent leads is a dark room because you are a budding photographer. Develop your prints, your eye, and your discipline, and see if you can become the next Margaret Bourke-White or Diane Arbus or Annie Leibovitz. Maybe the dark place where your talent leads is a desk where you will write in silence and solitude while classmates are outside cheerleading or shooting hoops. If you want to write, love to write, have to write, then write. Maybe the dark place where your talent leads is the stage—before the curtain goes up and the lights go on. If you want to dance and act and sing, now is the time to work on your skills.

"Talent is like electricity," Maya Angelou once said. "We don't understand electricity. We use it."

You don't yet know what your talents are? That's okay. Keep reaching, branching out. Be ready to recognize your strong suits.

I will forgive myself if I fail,
but I won't forgive myself if I don't try.

126

This thing we call ``failure'' is not the falling down,
but the staying down.

Mary Pickford

*M*iles Davis said, "Do not fear mistakes—there are none." Some teachers may think Davis was mistaken. Was he? Instead of fearing mistakes, learn from them. Do you always play it safe? If you take no risks, you play no riffs. Or as Sophia Loren put it, "Mistakes are part of the dues one pays for a full life."

No one is good at everything. Maybe your spelling is weak, yet your vocabulary is vast. Or maybe geometry is hard for you, yet you have more literary insights than your geometry teacher ever will. As Will Rogers wrote, "Everybody is ignorant, only on different subjects." Instead of being wowed or cowed by others, or self-conscious because you once repeated a year or did summer school, celebrate your strengths and work on what you need to work on. Move up a row in class, use spell check and dictionaries, take notes and review them, proofread your work, keep assignment pads, ask for a tutor, persevere. You can excel in the course you're best at, and you can improve in the one that you find most difficult.

I can be a good student
even if I'm not the best student.

*I would prefer even to fail with honor
than to win by cheating.*

Sophocles

The problem with cheating is that sooner or later you get caught. You may get caught by a proctor who then flunks, suspends, or expels you. Or you may get away with cheating, only to find that French or math gets harder and harder. If you can't conjugate *avoir* in the present, you can't do the *passé composé*. If you never learn multiplication, you will trip over simple equations all through high school—and maybe when ordering supplies for the class picnic—or, worse, when trying to keep a job that requires basic math skills. Try to stay on top of your lessons so that you can work independently and well. Don't panic, prepare.

What if someone is trying to copy your work? You don't need to tattle on cheaters, but you don't need to help them, either (especially when they are so good at helping themselves). You can cover your answers discreetly with your hand or arm or paper. Be proud of yourself for realizing that you are in school to learn, not to pretend to be learning. And be proud that you are not compromising your self-respect—which is something cheaters cannot crib.

*Knowing I can do it
beats hoping I can copy it.*

128

The happiest day in my life occurred when I found out I was dyslexic.

Ennis Cosby

Some students get poor grades because they don't take classes seriously or because they have major distractions or troubles at home. Others work hard, yet their teachers still complain that they are underachievers. If your grades don't reflect your effort and intelligence, ask your parents or a guidance counselor what you can do. You may need to improve your organizational skills. You may need tutoring or summer classes. Or you may have a learning disability. If you have dyslexia or attention deficit disorder, a medication or a new approach to learning may make all the difference. Instead of being frustrated, you can figure out how to make learning easier. And you can accept yourself, whether your added challenges are large or small. Helen Keller, who was blind, deaf, and confident, said, "I thank God for my handicaps, for, through them, I have found myself, my work, and my God."

What if it's not you but a friend or a family member who has a learning or other disability? It may take more patience than you thought you had, but try to be understanding. Never tease anyone for her differences.

Disabilities are a given.
Insensitivity is a choice.

129

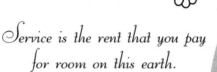

*Service is the rent that you pay
for room on this earth.*

Shirley Chisholm

People sign up to volunteer for all sorts of reasons. To have fun. To make friends. To help others. To improve skills. Even to show a college dean of admissions that they aren't just run-of-the-mill applicants—they're artistic, athletic, academic triple threats with a penchant for saving the world.

Are you interested in a cause that isn't offered in your school? Do you want to collect coats for the homeless or tutor disadvantaged kids or teach English as a second language? "Human history," wrote Julio Cortázar, "is the sad result of each one looking out for himself." Pearl Bailey lamented, "Everybody wants to do something to help, but nobody wants to be the first." Are you willing to initiate? See if you can talk others into caring about your crusade. See if you can start a community service of your own.

"After all, what's a life, anyway?" asks Charlotte, E. B. White's altruistic arachnid. "We're born, we live a little while, we die. . . . By helping you, perhaps I was trying to lift up my life a trifle. Heaven knows everyone's life can stand a little of that."

Helping you helps me, too.

*The one nice thing about sports
is that they prove men do have emotions
and are not afraid to show them.*

Jane O'Reilly

There are lots of good things about sports, and after-school sports are becoming more and more popular. "Jumping has always been the thing for me. It's like leaping for joy," says Olympic medalist Jackie Joyner-Kersee. Have you found a physical activity—basketball, soccer, track, gymnastics—that you love? Sports help kids make friends, stay fit, and enjoy a sense of belonging. Earl Woods said of his son Tiger, "I was using golf to teach him about life. About how to handle responsibility and pressure." Sports can also teach you about team spirit and group effort. Basketball coach Pat Riley cautions against succumbing to "the disease of me"—helping yourself instead of the team.

Maybe your favorite extracurricular activity is neither a do-good cause nor a team sport. Maybe you stay after school for chorus or band or chess or stage crew or theater or student council or yearbook committee or Latin Club. No matter what group has you taking the late bus home, being involved beats imagining that you have nothing to do. Being active beats being idle.

It's better to juggle than to sit on my hands.

From there to here,
from here to there,
funny things
are everywhere.

Dr. Seuss

ored? You don't get bored, do you? Restless, tired,
weary, challenged, taxed: okay. But not bored. As
Robert Louis Stevenson wrote, *"The world is so full of a
number of things, / I'm sure we should all be as happy as
kings."*

Not every moment in and out of school will be exciting,
but if you're often bored, shake up your routine. Be creative and resourceful, and figure out what you can add to
your life. Different activities? Different friends? Turn off
the television. Put down the unthrilling thriller. Close the
refrigerator door. If you get bored, get busy. Because as
Eloise, the precocious little girl who lives at the Plaza
Hotel says, "Getting bored is not allowed."

See if you can add something new to your week as well
as get more interested in what you are already doing. Keep
your energy up. "Is giving yourself a pep talk every day
silly, superficial, childish? No, on the contrary," wrote
Dale Carnegie, "it is the very essence of sound
psychology.

Boredom is beneath me.

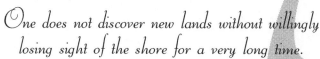

One does not discover new lands without willingly losing sight of the shore for a very long time.

André Gide

It took guts for Columbus to sail the ocean blue. But he did it. Now American students routinely travel abroad for summers, semesters, junior years. Some programs, such as the Experiment in International Living and School Year Abroad, arrange for students to live with families in other countries.

Curious about Costa Rica, Canada, China? You decide how far you want to go in terms of language, distance, and culture.

Adults who have jobs and families can't just pick up and take off. You can. Query your teachers and guidance counselors. Short on funds? Save allowances and earnings and apply for scholarships. When you return, your school and friends will still be there. But you will have new friends, perspectives, and language skills. And no one can take your memories or your adventure away from you. In a Julius Alvarez novel, a character recalls: "These baby monkeys were kept in a cage so long, they wouldn't come out when the doors were finally left open."

Come out. Explore. Let the Earth be your classroom. As Mark Twain wrote, "I have never let my schooling interfere with my education."

To move forward, I have to let go.

Work

Work is more fun than fun.

Noel Coward

People who are really lucky love working and would keep working even if they won the lottery and could retire. But many are not so lucky. Many don't like their jobs at all and dread going to work each day.

"Work is not man's punishment. It is his reward and his strength, his glory and his pleasure," wrote George Sand. Everyone likes weekends and vacations, but if you are among the fortunate few for whom work is a passion, then someday you can look forward to Mondays as much as Saturdays. (Well, almost.)

For years, near strangers have probably been asking you what you were going to be when you grew up. What did you answer? Singer? Doctor? Ballerina? Teacher? Actress? Firefighter? Have you changed your mind since then? When you're young, you can change your mind again and again as you get to know your interests and your strengths. As you think about possible careers, consider these words of Whoopi Goldberg: "There are many, many tense adults—we don't need any more tense adults . . . make sure you remember who you are and all the stuff that's made you laugh and dance and jump around."

Work may be a four-letter word, but it can spell satisfaction.

*Work is something you can count on, a trusted,
lifelong friend who never deserts you.*

Margaret Bourke-White

If you enjoy taking photographs or playing the harp or writing letters or doing math or meeting new people or traveling or helping others, you can enjoy these pleasures all your life. If you can manage to turn your pleasures into a way of making money, you are blessed indeed. Every job has pros and cons, good days and bad days. Work itself has a bad name. But putting your skills to use builds pride.

What are you good at? What do you like to do? Slowly but surely you can aim toward work that interests you. Your future career can be more than a way to make a living; it can be a way to enjoy life.

"Work and love—these are the basics," said George Santayana. "If you rest, you rust," said Helen Hayes. Without love, life can seem pretty bleak. But without work, even leisure can feel long. Work—whether at school or at a job—can provide structure, focus, meaning, and comfort to your days.

It feels good to work hard.

Work spares us from three great evils:
boredom, vice, and need.

Voltaire

Whether your first job is minding children, waiting tables, or selling jeans, you are learning more than you may realize. If you baby-sit, you're not only perfecting the art of putting on Pampers, you're learning about responsibility and punctuality and how to negotiate money with parents and bedtime with kids. If you're waiting tables, you're sharpening math, memory, and people skills. If you're selling clothes, you're mastering presentation, time management, and how to get along with customers and co-workers. You may also be learning that you don't want to baby-sit or wait tables or ring up sales forever.

Today, your real work may be to do your best at school. In the future, you may work to make money, develop expertise, meet people, help others, realize dreams. Whether you take on a part-time summer job, a volunteer internship, or a full-time paid position, work is one of the ways in which you define your life. Louisa May Alcott wrote: "Work is and has always been my salvation and I thank the Lord for it."

Work is the meat and potatoes of life.

I have the same goal I've had ever since I was a girl. I want to rule the world.

Madonna

Are you ambitious? Not everyone is. Some people are more like Ferdinand the bull. Remember him? Ferdinand didn't want to be the fiercest bull in the bull-ring. He wanted to sit under the cork tree and smell the flowers. And why not?

If, however, you do have larger aspirations, dream them, own them, live them. "I always knew I wanted to be somebody," wrote artist Faith Ringgold. "I think that's where it begins."

Do you want to be somebody? Who? What are your heroines like? What do you enjoy doing now that you think you will always enjoy doing?

No matter how big or how small your goals, keep moving forward. "It's never too late to be what you might have been," wrote George Eliot. And as President John F. Kennedy put it, "Once you say you're going to settle for second, that's what happens to you in life, I find."

Dreams are like live coals.
I can let them cool into ash,
or I can fan them until they burn brightly.

If you want a place in the sun, you've got to put up with a few blisters.

Abigail Van Buren

No one ever said it was easy. If you want something, you have to go after it. Don't wait for the phone to ring. Pick up the receiver yourself. Tell people who you are and what you can do and how you can help them. A lucky break may come your way, but if no one hands you the perfect job, your job is to go out and find it.

Roseanne said, "The thing women have got to learn is that nobody gives you power. You just take it." Lauren Bacall said, "The world doesn't owe you a damn thing." Harsh words? Yes. But the point is that if you want to be an actress, a tennis star, a composer, or an entrepreneur, it's up to you, not the rest of the world, to make that happen. Put in the time and energy. Pay your dues. Ask yourself what you are willing to give up to get what you want. As the Chinese say, "Talk does not cook rice."

I can climb any ladder, rung by rung.

Luck is a matter of preparation meeting opportunity.
Oprah Winfrey

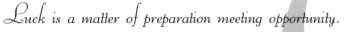

*E*very so often, seemingly out of the blue, opportunity will knock. It may not announce itself in an obvious way. It won't say, "Here I am! Your long-awaited opportunity of a lifetime!" It may be far more subtle. Your teacher or neighbor or parent or aunt will make a comment, and suddenly you will realize that there's a job opening (maybe without pay) or a chance to live in Florence (maybe only as a baby-sitter). Or perhaps the lead in the school musical or soprano in the choir or captain of the hockey team will be absent the day of a performance or game, and you will realize (even before the director or coach) that you can save the day—and strut your stuff. Is this a time for modesty, true or false? No. This is a time for action!

Ann Landers wrote, "Opportunities are usually disguised as hard work, so most people don't recognize them." Can you recognize them and take advantage of them? To quote a German proverb: "God gives the nuts, but he does not crack them." Do what it takes to become lucky. Because while success does not simply boil down to who you know, whom you *get* to know can make all the difference.

When opportunity knocks,
I'll have my shoes on.

142

Shoot for the moon. Even if you miss it, you will land among the stars.

Les Brown

Aim high. Try hard. Have faith. Montel Williams writes, "If you have faith, you can move mountains. If you have faith in something bigger than yourself—God, community, family, whatever—then anything is possible."

Why not stand up for your convictions? Or sit down for them. Remember Rosa Parks? The black woman who refused to give up her seat to a white man on a bus in Alabama. She recalled, "He asked if I was going to stand up, and I said, 'No, I'm not.' And he said, 'Well, if you don't stand up, I'm going to . . . call the police and have you arrested.' I said, 'You may do that.'" Next thing you know, she'd quietly started the Montgomery Bus Boycott—and made Civil Rights history.

Aviator Amelia Earhart, a headstrong heroine, wrote in a letter: "Please know that I am quite aware of the hazards. I want to do it because I want to do it. Women must try to do things as men have tried. When they fail, their failure must be but a challenge to others."

It is better to assume success than to fear failure.

143

What's terrible is to pretend that the second-rate is first-rate. To pretend that you don't need love when you do; or you like your work when you know quite well you're capable of better.

Doris Lessing

Keep your standards high. You may be so good at a certain subject that you can turn in quick work for a great grade. But if you're not an ace at science, isn't that all the more reason to put in extra energy and dazzle yourself as well as the teacher?

"I remember a very important lesson that my father gave me when I was twelve or thirteen," recalls Nobel Prize winner Toni Morrison. "He said, 'You know, today I welded a perfect seam and I signed my name to it.' And I said, 'But, Daddy, no one's going to see it!' And he said, 'Yeah, but I know it's there.'"

Whether you're baking a pie, washing dishes, running a race, writing a paper, multiplying fractions, conducting a science experiment, or welding a seam, why do less than your best? Sign your work with pride. And when you do make a mistake, ask yourself what you can learn from it.

I bet I can do even better.

Gardens are not made by singing,
"Oh how beautiful!"
and sitting in the shade.

Rudyard Kipling

*D*reams help you think big. But thinking big is not enough. "It's plain hard work that does it," wrote inventor Thomas Edison. "Genius," he explained, "is one percent inspiration and ninety-nine percent perspiration."

It helps to be as brilliant as Edison. But even Edison had to buckle down. If you spend time and thought on an essay, it will probably be better than if you dash it off on the school bus. If you study for the math test, you'll probably do better than if you take it cold.

Working hard pays off, whether as a salary, a colorful garden, a historic invention, or better grades. As Mary Pipher wrote in *Reviving Ophelia*, "Often what hurts in the short term is ultimately rewarding, while what feels good in the short term is ultimately punishing." When you work hard, it shows. So take the advice Yoda gives Luke Skywalker in *The Empire Strikes Back*: "Do—or do not. There is no try."

If I want to make a difference,
I have to make an effort.

145

Nothing in the world will take the place of persistence. Talent will not; nothing is more common than unsuccessful men with talent. Genius will not; unrewarded genius is almost a proverb. Education will not; the world is full of educated derelicts.

Calvin Coolidge

Persistence and determination are your skeleton keys—the keys that can open any door. Remember the busy mice in the Cinderella movie? Remember how they sang, "We can do it, we can do it, there is really nothing to it"? Remember the blue train in *The Little Engine That Could*? Remember how it huffed and puffed uphill while repeating: "I think I can I think I can I think I can?" Remember the tortoise and the hare in the Aesop story? Remember how slow and steady won the race? Remember Phil in Disney's *Hercules* and how he told our hero, "Giving up is for rookies"?

If you give up, it's Game Over. So don't give up. As Josh Billings wrote, "Consider the postage stamp: its usefulness consists in the ability to stick to one thing till it gets there."

If I don't believe in myself, why should others believe in me?

146

Just don't give up trying to do what you really want to do. Where there's love and inspiration, I don't think you can go wrong.

Ella Fitzgerald

Give up? You're just getting started. Achievement comes with struggle. The rich and famous all tell stories about the rejections that paved their way. So don't let naysayers or jealous friends block your path. As Mark Twain warned, "Keep away from people who try to belittle your ambitions. Small people always do that, but the really great make you feel that you, too, can become great."

Success won't happen overnight. But if you already know you want to star in a Broadway musical or vault with the Olympic gymnastics team or find a cure for cancer or write the definitive Great American Novel, go to it. Joseph Campbell wrote, "Follow your bliss." Laura Schlessinger wrote, "Dreams are just unrealized goals." Bill Clinton said, "Dream big and chase your dreams." Sure, it's wise to be realistic. But it's foolish to compromise or back down too soon.

The mountain looks tall, but I will scale many mountains.

In Monroeville, well . . . if they know you are working at home, they think nothing of walking right in for coffee. But they wouldn't dream of interrupting you on the golf course.

Harper Lee

If you care about what you are reading or writing or memorizing or practicing or learning, why should you put up with endless interruptions? Yes, you have to stop for dinnertime and bedtime. But you don't have to put down your pen or shut down the computer for every phone call or visitor. Let an answering machine or a family member record your phone calls, and return them later. Don't be afraid to tell a visitor that it's a bad time and say when would be better. You're allowed to take your work seriously; most people will even admire you for it.

As Robert Frost wrote, "The best way out is always through." So minimize distractions and barrel forward. If a deadline or a test or a performance is upon you, work is your top priority. Schedule visits with friends afterward. You'll have more fun because you'll be more relaxed.

I don't have to apologize for taking myself seriously.

In the face of an obstacle which is impossible to overcome, stubbornness is stupid.

Simone de Beauvoir

*P*ersistence and effort count for a lot, but if it's time to bail, it's okay to bail. "There is a difference between being convinced and being stubborn," wrote Maya Angelou. "If you butt your head against a stone wall long enough, at some point you realize the wall is stone and that your head is flesh and blood."

If you've spent two years in a painfully unrequited crush, enough already. *¡Basta y sobra!* If you've invested four years in ballet lessons but they're no longer fun and you're not destined to be a dancer and there are other fields you'd like to explore, be glad for the arabesques but go ahead and cut loose so you can explore and enjoy other endeavors.

To quote from *The Wizard of Oz*: " 'It must be inconvenient to be made of flesh,' said the scarecrow, thoughtfully, 'for you must sleep and eat and drink. However, you have brains, and it is worth a lot of bother to be able to think properly.' " Think properly. Don't believe that giving up is always bad. Giving up one goal may make it possible for you to attain another goal.

I can use my brain—and my common sense.

Notice the difference between what happens when a man says to himself, "I have failed three times," and what happens when he says, "I am a failure."

S. I. Hayakawa

*E*veryone messes up. But when you fall short of your goal, you don't have to roll over and play dead. You can get up and keep moving—and give yourself credit for having tried in the first place. Sometimes experience is worth more than a trophy. And as George Eliot wrote: "Failure after long perseverance is much grander than never to have a striving good enough to be called a failure."

Adjust your expectations when necessary, but keep trying for long shots. You'll never get the lead if you don't audition. You'll never make the team if you don't try out. If you don't risk rejection, you don't risk success. Ask for what you want and go after it. "The common idea that success spoils people by making them vain, egotistical, and self-complacent is erroneous," wrote Somerset Maugham. "On the contrary, it makes them, for the most part, humble, tolerant, and kind. Failure makes people cruel and bitter."

If my goal is still ahead, I have not failed.

Woman must not depend upon the protection of man, but must be taught to protect herself.

Susan B. Anthony

"Summer afternoon—summer afternoon; to me these have always been the most beautiful words in the English language," wrote Henry James. Dorothy Parker begged to differ. "The two most beautiful words in the English language," she quipped, "are 'check enclosed.'"

Work may be its own reward, but it is good to get paid. And it is important to know how to make money.

Many girls set out to have careers. Others hope to marry men who will be the breadwinners. This plan may pan out . . . but what if the hard-working husband loses his job or dies or asks for a divorce? What if he turns into a cheat or a beast, and the wife wants out? Divorce isn't pretty no matter how you look at it. But divorce with poverty is worse.

Many women remain single or become single, and unless they are born rich, they need to know how to hold down a job and support themselves.

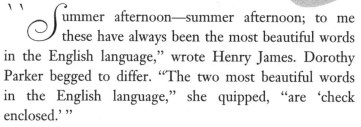

*If I know how to spend money,
I had better learn how to make money.*

Ask a lot but take what is offered.

Russian proverb

When you baby-sit or shovel snow or take care of a neighbor's pets or help her clean out her garage, what do you say when she asks, "What do you charge"? Do you shrug, blush, and mumble, "Whatever"? Next time, find out what the going rate is, ask parents and friends for advice, and decide ahead what the job is worth to you. Then name your price: "Ten dollars" or "Twenty dollars" or "Three dollars per hour" or "Six dollars per hour." Be reasonable but sound definite. An employer can always make a counteroffer.

Many people feel awkward about money. Their voices become quiet or high; their sentences sound like questions. But a good worker should be compensated for her labor. Your employer may even respect you more when she sees that you respect yourself and value your time.

During his inaugural address, President John F. Kennedy, speaking on a grander scale, said, "Let us never negotiate out of fear, but let us never fear to negotiate."

I will ask for what I think I deserve.

Shopping seemed to take an entirely too important place in women's lives. You never saw men milling around in men's departments. . . . I used to wonder if shopping was a form of escape for women who had no worthwhile interests.

Mary Barnett Gilson

There's nothing wrong with shopping. But the mall is not the be-all and end-all. In Arthur Miller's play *The Price*, a character says, "Years ago a person, he was unhappy, didn't know what to do with himself—he'd go to church, start a revolution—*something*. Today you're unhappy? Can't figure it out? What is the salvation? Go shopping."

Is Miller describing you? Do you spend all your time and money in stores? Some teenagers ruin their credit ratings by mistaking credit cards for blank checks. Others flash debit cards—and abracadabra—their savings disappear.

When you do shop, be careful. Take advantage of sales, but if the shirt is no-return, make sure it fits and has no missing buttons. No matter how cute, patient, or insistent the clerk is, if you don't want it, don't buy it. And at the grocer's, check expiration dates. Why spend today's money on yesterday's milk?

I won't spend big money on little nothings.

Save money and money will save you.

Jamaican proverb

"I've been rich and I've been poor. Rich is better," said Sophie Tucker. Most everyone would agree. It's good to have money and to know how to make more.

Yet the Bible says, "The love of money is the root of all evil." If money starts complicating your relationships or compromising your values, that's not good. Borrowing or lending money can sabotage friendships. And choosing friends because they are rich is shallow indeed.

Do wealthy people have the most fun? Not necessarily. Tennis champion Martina Navratilova points out, "The rich guys buy a football team, the poor guys buy a football. It's all relative."

If you have no dollars to spare, it can be hard to believe that rich people aren't happy all the time. But rich people can get used to caviar and fancy cars as fast as the rest of us can get used to hot dogs and bicycles. And rich people, like all people, have worries, troubles, and unfulfilled dreams of their own.

While money opens up certain possibilities, it does not define who you are. While money helps, it cannot buy time or love or happiness.

The bottom line is important but so is the rest of the page.

The trouble with being in the rat race is that even if you win, you're still a rat.

Lily Tomlin

Money is a motivator, and right now you might do backflips just to land a job at minimum wage. Fine. Once you're hired, don't get fired. Work efficiently and independently. Speak up if you don't understand a task. Accept responsibility if you make a mistake. Be friendly; give compliments; say thank-you to your boss, co-workers, and customers. And don't bound out the door at five sharp as though you're a puppy who has to piddle. As coach Vince Lombardi said, "If you aren't fired with enthusiasm, you will be fired with enthusiasm."

Let's say you're such a good worker that you get promoted and promoted and promoted. Congratulations! But you should still keep an eye on the big picture. Is this your chosen field? Even if you make a lot of money, be sure you enjoy how you make it. As Maurice Sendak wrote, "There must be more to life than having everything." And as Paul Simon said, "Fame is a very dangerous acquisition. Don't waste your time pursuing it. If you do get it, use it to help others. Otherwise it can be poisonous."

I can balance what I have to do with what I want to do.

155

Many a man thinks he is making something when he's only changing things around.

Zora Neale Hurston

Can you make your work more meaningful? Can you earn the affection and respect of your co-workers? If you believe in what you do, and you do it well and with gusto, you will energize yourself and those around you. "Every calling is great when greatly pursued," remarked Oliver Wendell Holmes, Jr. Do you have a calling? A worthwhile goal?

As a child you might have read Barbara Cooney's *Miss Rumphius*. It's about an old woman who, remembering a conversation with her grandfather, thinks, "But there is still one more thing I have to do. I have to make the world more beautiful." And she does. She plants the fields and hillsides of her seaside home with blue- and purple- and rose-colored lupines that bloom beautifully year after year after year.

Madeline Albright, the first woman Secretary of State, put it this way: "We have a responsibility in our time, as others have had in theirs, not to be prisoners of history, but to shape history."

The world is not perfect;
I can try to make it better.

Work while you work,
Play while you play;
One thing each time,
That is the way.

McGuffey Reader

All work and no play makes Jack a dull boy—and it doesn't do much for Jill, either. Give yourself a break. If you love to read and write, you still have to get some sunshine and hang out with friends. If you love your after-school job, you still have to attend to your family and the rest of your life. Study breaks and work breaks aren't perks—they're necessities! "The time you enjoy wasting is not wasted time," wrote Bertrand Russell. "A little rebellion is a good thing," wrote Thomas Jefferson.

When you work, work hard. But afterward, relax. There is no need to burn yourself out or to meet impossible standards or to make tons of money. You don't have to pay the rent yet, right? Don't pressure yourself if you don't have to. Chill out. Take walks. Take naps. Call friends. You're entitled to gather your rosebuds as well as your report cards and paychecks.

You're getting stressed, overwhelmed, exhausted? Here's Lily Tomlin's remedy: "For fast-acting relief, try slowing down."

On the seventh day, even God put Her feet up.

Parting Words

An adult is an obsolete child.

Dr. Seuss

All children, except one, grow up. They soon know that they will grow up, and the way Wendy knew was this. One day when she was two years old, she was playing in a garden, and she plucked another flower and ran with it to her mother. I suppose she must have looked rather delightful, for Mrs. Darling put her hand to her heart and cried, "Oh, why can't you remain like this forever!" This was all that passed between them on the subject, but henceforth Wendy knew that she must grow up. You always know after you are two. Two is the beginning of the end.

So begins J. M. Barrie's *Peter Pan and Wendy*. And so begins the last chapter of this book. Being a child is wonderful, but being your age can be even better. You're old enough to pick your own music and friends and activities. Yet you're not too old to enjoy cartwheels, cartoons, revolving doors, banana splits, rainbows, kittens, even snowball fights. And why should you ever be?

In 1897, an eight-year-old girl wrote the editor of *The New York Sun* and asked, "Is there a Santa Claus?" His wise reply: "Yes, Virginia, there is a Santa Claus. He exists as certainly as love and generosity and devotion exist . . . how dreary would be the world if there were no Santa Claus!"

I can grow up, not old.

A child's world is fresh and new and beautiful, full of wonder and excitement. It is our misfortune that for most of us, that clear-eyed vision, that true instinct for what is beautiful and awe-inspiring, is dimmed and even lost before we reach adulthood.

Rachel Carson

When was the last time you looked at a tree or a leaf or a flower or even a work of art and were astounded by its beauty? When is the last time you looked at the world with a child's eyes—or even a tourist's eyes—and felt surprised and uplifted?

In E. B. White's *Charlotte's Web*, everyone gives advice to Wilbur the pig. The spider says, "Slowly, slowly! Never hurry and never worry!" The goose says, "Run all over! Skip and dance, jump and prance! . . . The world is a wonderful place when you're young."

The world is a wonderful place no matter how old you are. But it helps if you can retain your sense of wonder and remember to skip and dance. "I finally figured out the only reason to be alive is to enjoy it," wrote Rita Mae Brown.

I will enjoy the time of my life.

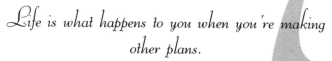

Life is what happens to you when you're making other plans.

John Lennon

Patricia MacLachlan wrote in a novel, "He never learned that most things are only there for a moment, quite perfect and fine, like snow." Have you learned that some things don't last? Beautiful things, like snowflakes. Awful things, like rumors.

Do you notice your surroundings? Do you enjoy your routine—and the moments that break up your routine? Do you love your family? Your friends? The stuff of your life? Do you relish what you have instead of always yearning for more?

"One cannot collect all the beautiful shells on the beach. One can collect only a few, and they are the more beautiful if they are few," wrote Anne Morrow Lindbergh. This Yiddish proverb strikes a grimmer note: "Shrouds are made without pockets." Translation: You can't take it with you. But you can enjoy yourself today, can't you?

I will not just be alive; I will be aware.

Seize the day.

Horace

Do you know people who say "I can't wait until Thanksgiving" or "I can't wait until I'm older"? No matter how bright your future, why wish away today? Do you know people who say "Thank God it's Friday" or "I have an hour to kill"? Why dismiss Monday, Tuesday, Wednesday, and Thursday? Why kill time when you can't make more of it?

"Youth is wasted on the young," George Bernard Shaw wrote. But not your youth. You're paying attention to your life. And while it's impossible to live each day to the fullest, to enjoy each hour to the hilt, to make each minute count, you recognize that as a worthy goal. "Today is always gone tomorrow," wrote Wislawa Szymborska, a Polish poet who won the Nobel Prize.

Do you find time for fun and for work? For pleasure and for purpose? You can't do it all, but you can do what you can. And even if you have only five minutes, you can read, make a call, check your homework, set the table—or grab a catnap.

Seize the day . . . squeeze the moment.

Being an artist means, not reckoning and counting, but ripening like the tree which does not force its sap. . . . I learn it daily, learn it with patience to which I am grateful: patience is everything!

Rainer Maria Rilke

Patience is everything whether you are an artist or not. You can't rush puberty or prom night or summer vacation or Christmas or Hanukkah or friendship or fitness or love or happiness or wisdom. You can try to move in the right direction. You can try to stay healthy and strong. You can try to make your days meaningful and to listen to the YES inside and outside you. But you can't hurry your life along. So why not savor it?

As Ursula K. LeGuin put it, "It is good to have an end to journey toward; but it is the journey that matters, in the end." And Adlai Stevenson wrote, "It's not the years in your life but the life in your years that counts." Thomas Beller put it this way: "I have no trouble getting older, I just want to take my time about it."

Learning patience requires patience.

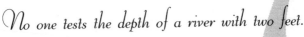

No one tests the depth of a river with two feet.

African proverb

*D*oing things carefully and well makes more sense than doing things in a slapdash way, impulsively, or incorrectly. "Better to ask twice than lose your way once," goes a Danish proverb.

Better, too, to leave an extra fifteen minutes to get to the airport than to sweat out every red light. Even if you're just going to a movie or meeting friends, leave early so you arrive on time. Bring a book or your diary or some postcards; if you get there first, you can always read or write.

You can choose to be punctual, not frantic; organized, not overwhelmed. Piet Hein wrote a poem that could be engraved on too many tombstones:

> *Here lies, extinguished in his prime,*
> *a victim of modernity:*
> *but yesterday he hadn't time—*
> *and now he has eternity.*

I will give myself the time I need.

I never travel without my diary. One should always have something sensational to read in the train.

Oscar Wilde

Do you have a diary? A diary is a friend who listens, and writing down your thoughts and observations can help you discover what matters to you—and help you keep things in perspective. Are you worried that you're penning drivel or just whining on paper? Keep writing. Your best words will come. A diary accepts both self-pity and brilliant insights. Are you worried instead about privacy? Trust your family—but hide your diary!

Someday you may look back on your diary with embarrassment. Is that the best you could spell? Did you really have a crush on *him*? Don't discard old diaries. Reread them. They'll show the arc of who you were and who you have become. Revisiting one's childhood and adolescence is one of the worthy diversions of adulthood. Plato wrote, "The life which is unexamined is not worth living." Milan Kundera asked, "You think that just because it's already happened, the past is finished and unchangeable? Oh no, the past is cloaked in multicolored taffeta and every time we look at it we see a different hue."

I can time travel through my own life.

Into each life, some rain must fall,
Some days must be dark and dreary.

Henry Wadsworth Longfellow

Nothing is perfect, and bad hair days (as well as true travails) are inevitable. As Dolly Parton puts it, "If you want the rainbow, you gotta put up with the rain."

But dreary days help us appreciate bright ones. Because things are terrible today doesn't mean that they will stay terrible. Sometimes you have to undergo arduous training to achieve a fabulous performance. Sometimes you have to survive a wrenching breakup to get to the winning relationship.

If you bomb a test, that doesn't mean you'll flunk the course. If your friends turn on you, that doesn't mean you'll spend your life alone. Even if there is real heartbreak, there will still be joys ahead.

Someday you may even be able to convert your worst experiences into art. As John Ciardi wrote, "You don't have to suffer to be a poet. Adolescence is enough suffering for anyone." As a character in an A.R. Gurney play puts it, "Life has taught me this: even if the main course is somewhat disappointing, there's always dessert."

Without rain and bees . . . no flowers.

I like living. I have sometimes been wildly, despairingly, acutely miserable, racked with sorrow, but through it all I still know quite certainly that just to be alive is a grand thing.

Agatha Christie

Things will look different tomorrow. Things will be better soon. There are adults who can help you. If you want to change your life, you can. And as Alice Walker put it: "Life is better than death, I believe, if only because it is less boring, and because it has fresh peaches in it."

Everybody despairs at some point. As Calderón de la Barca wrote, "No unhappiness is equal to that of anticipating unhappiness." But people forgive; new friends and boyfriends come along; situations turn out better than you thought they would. You are also more resilient than you think you are. You have inner resources that you haven't yet tapped. Albert Camus wrote, "In the midst of winter, I finally learned that there was in me an invincible summer."

Time alone can make a difference. "If Winter comes," Percy Bysshe Shelley asked, "can Spring be far behind?"

Moods are like seasons: They change.

Regret is an appalling waste of energy; you can't build on it; it's only good for wallowing in.

Katherine Mansfield

Edith Piaf, a tiny French singer, belted out, "*Je ne regrette rien* (I regret nothing)." William Maxwell, when nearing ninety, wrote, "I have regrets but there are not very many of them and, fortunately, I forget what they are."

Everyone sifts through memories. Some people regret things they said or did. Others regret things they didn't say or do. If you have a habit of second-guessing yourself, make an effort to learn from the past but to connect to the present. "Life must be understood backwards," wrote Søren Kierkegaard, "but . . . it must be lived forwards." Consider this verse by Piet Hein:

> *The road to wisdom? —Well, it's plain*
> *and simple to express:*
>> *Err*
>> *And err*
>> *And err again*
>> *But less*
>> *And less*
>> *And less.*

I can look back, but I will move forward.

If I have lost the ring, I still have the fingers.

Italian proverb

There is always another way of looking at things. Deep in the Hundred Acre Wood, Winnie the Pooh was once planning to give Eeyore a jar of honey for his birthday. But the chubby cubby got hungry and licked the jar clean before realizing his mistake. Did he feel awful? No. Ever the optimist, Pooh examined the empty jar and said, "I'm very glad that I thought of giving you a Useful Pot to put things in." Eeyore was glad, too. What he wanted, after all, was just to be remembered on his birthday.

Yes, you're bummed that you lost your five-dollar bill. But think how pleased the person who finds it will be. Yes, you're upset that you lost your prized blue ribbon. But you'll never forget what it felt like to win.

You can't always give troubles a positive spin. But when things look bleak, look again. Many sorry situations work out for the best. Shift your camera angle and you might find something to salvage—or even celebrate.

I will ask myself:
Is there another way of looking at this?

171

Do not be breakin' a shin on a stool that's not in your path.

Irish proverb

*D*o you invent problems? Are you an alarmist? If you can't find your keys or glasses or purse, they probably aren't lost forever. They're probably on the bureau in the next room. If your sister is ten minutes late returning from the store, she probably didn't have a car accident. She probably ran one more errand.

Your life has enough stress without your creating more. If you're going out with someone you like, why obsess that he might break up with you? If you're a good student, why worry that the next test will do you in? Why cry yourself to sleep over an ex-friend or a lost crush? It makes more sense to dry your eyes and make more friends—female and male.

The Italians have a proverb: "There is no rose without thorns." It's true—even the Lady Banksia rose, which is called thornless, has tiny thorns. But why be so anxious about thorns that you overlook a rose's beauty and fragrance? And if ever you do have a thorn in your side, just take it out and toss it away.

I will not worry unnecessarily or panic prematurely.

If you live in squalor, you have to have order.

Quentin Crisp

Is your room so tidy it could be photographed? Skip this page. Is your room a disaster area (even if you know where the essentials are)? Take action.

Matsushita Konosuke, founder of Panasonic, said, "It is necessary to approach a project with the conviction that it *can* be done, and not waste energy worrying about its difficulty." Instead of despairing because your room is beyond-belief messy, start straightening it up. It's a big job, but it's doable.

Once you decide to organize rather than agonize, tackle the task methodically. Begin by making your bed in the morning—you can do it when you're still half asleep. Sort through drawers one at a time, putting away or throwing away the contents. What's that pile on your desk? Move it to the kitchen table and decide which papers go where. You've outgrown some clothes? Toss them or give them away. You want to save last year's reports? Okay, but must they be front and center in your work space? Take action and file, file, file!

It's as easy to drape your jeans over a hanger as it is to drape them over a chair.

173

Television has proved that people will look at anything rather than at each other.

Ann Landers

"It rots the senses in the head! It kills imagination dead!" wrote Roald Dahl. "Television is chewing gum for the eyes," wrote Frank Lloyd Wright. "Television is an invention that permits you to be entertained in your living room by people you wouldn't have in your home," wrote David Frost.

Television isn't all bad. There are nature programs, documentaries, sitcoms, and other shows that help you learn and laugh and relax. Nonetheless, as Lily Tomlin points out, "If you read a lot, you're considered well-read. But if you watch a lot of TV, you're not considered well-viewed."

When is television a problem? When it's always on. When you find yourself watching whatever is offered rather than choosing particular programs. When you start to want what commercials tell you to want. When you blow off doing homework or playing sports because it's easier to sprawl on the couch. When you can't think of anything to do with a friend besides watch a video. When you stop having friends because it's easier to have one-way relationships.

I can turn the TV on . . . and off.

174

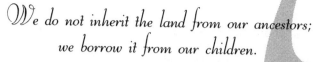

*We do not inherit the land from our ancestors;
we borrow it from our children.*

Native American proverb

"Earth's crammed with heaven," wrote Elizabeth Barrett Browning. "Hell is paved with good intentions," wrote Samuel Johnson. Many people mean well and are all for waving the green flag of ecology. Then they litter, reach for paper towels instead of a sponge, or let cashiers put tiny purchases into plastic bags instead of putting the item and receipt directly into their purse or backpack.

Even if you're not on a committee to save the rain forest, adopt a highway, or clean up city parks, you can do your part for the environment. "Something is better than nothing," wrote Lady Bird Johnson, a former First Lady and the founder of the National Wildflower Research Center. Every effort counts. Recycle. Think twice before buying Styrofoam cups or plastic forks, flushing the toilet for mere tissue, leaving lights on when you exit a room, turning up the heat when you could put on a sweater, blasting the air-conditioning when you could open a window. Perhaps your family can afford to use lots of products, water, and utilities. But the planet can't.

I won't be wasteful.

The Earth is crying out to us.
And so few of us are actually listening.

Stevie Wonder

You can't vote yet. But politics affect you. And your decisions and actions can have their effects, too. Reading the small print can make a big difference. Study the label on a can of tuna. Were nets used that could harm dolphins? Find out. Does your grocer sell organically grown fruits and vegetables? The fewer pesticides out there, the better (for you *and* the world). Can you go for unbleached flour, recycled paper products, less heavily packaged foods? Newman's Own popcorn and Ben & Jerry's ice cream are as delicious as anyone else's, and those companies donate a portion of their earnings to philanthropic causes. Why not buy products from companies with a conscience? Why support businesses that use child labor when other businesses go out of their way to hire disadvantaged adults? Why support a huge corporation if you can get what you want at a small corner bookstore, pharmacy, or mom-and-pop diner? Is your money going where your values are? Write letters to politicians and executives. Inform your friends. Make your voice heard. "Whether you want it or not," wrote Wislawa Szymborska, "you walk with political steps on political ground."

I can be complacent—or committed.

We have just enough religion to make us hate, but not enough to make us love one another.

Jonathan Swift

Do you believe in God? Are you Catholic or Protestant or Jewish or Muslim or Buddhist? Is worship a part of your life?

Some people who are not religious mock those who are. And some devoutly religious people have zero tolerance for those who don't share their beliefs.

"The problem with writing about religion is that you run the risk of offending seriously religious people, and then they come after you with machetes," wrote humorist Dave Barry. "So I am going to be very sensitive, here, which is not easy, because the thing about religion is that everybody else's always appears stupid."

Cross yourself, keep kosher, bow to Mecca—or don't. But don't make fun of people who worship differently from you—or who don't worship at all. Respect and understanding are cornerstones of all religions and are important values whether you believe in God or not.

I can respect people who are different from me.

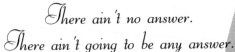

There ain't no answer.
There ain't going to be any answer.
There never has been an answer.
That's the answer.

Gertrude Stein

"Nothing in life is to be feared," wrote Marie Curie, a scientist and Nobel Prize winner. "It is only to be understood." But who understands everything? Not authors. Not therapists. Not teachers. Not principals. Not poets.

We can all try to understand ourselves and each other better. And some people do have more insight and sense than others. But there is no rule book, no answer sheet.

At times you may feel stymied. You may not know how to finish a painting or short story. Or where to go to college. Or which man to get serious with. More experienced friends, relatives, and teachers may offer opinions worth hearing. But the decision will be yours to make. East Coast or West Coast? David or Daniel? Door #1 or Door #2? Take your time making the important decisions. And try to take comfort in knowing that nothing is black and white. There can be more than one right answer. And you can change your mind.

Life is not algebra.

178

Don't try so much to form your character—it's like trying to pull open a rosebud. Live as you like best, and your character will form itself.

Henry James

Many people wade through life without making conscious choices. Many people live passively, with little reflection or curiosity. "To live is the rarest thing in the world," wrote Oscar Wilde. "Most people just exist."

You are not most people. You are taking the time to think and to consider the thoughts of wise (and otherwise) men and women born long before you. You are moving from confusion to confidence. And you are beginning to appreciate and believe in yourself.

"To be what we are, and to become what we are becoming, is the only end in life," wrote Robert Louis Stevenson.

I can try to lead my life instead of being led by it.

The ripest peach is on the highest tree.

James Whitcomb Riley

Some girls lose their balance during these fast-changing years. Others hit their stride. Think about what you want your life to be like. Who you want to be. What you want to accomplish.

"It's not enough to be industrious; so are the ants—what are you industrious about?" asked Henry David Thoreau. Many adults are set in their ways, entrenched in their careers. You are still free to choose your path.

If you have worthy goals, it will take time and energy to realize them. You have time and energy. Don't listen to naysayers. Squelch the voice inside you that whispers that you can't do it. You can do it. You can!

As Angus Wilson wrote, "Your willingness to wrestle with your demons will cause your angels to sing."

Are you willing to wrestle with your demons? Will you let your angels hit the high notes? Give it your all. Because life doesn't start at graduation. It has already started.

Watch out, world, here I come!

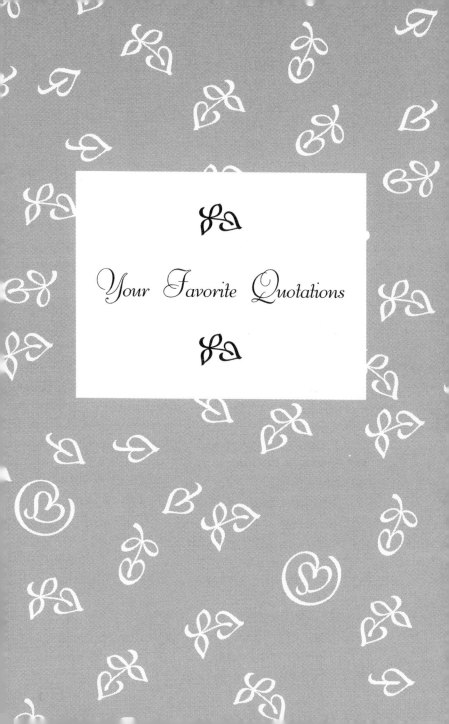

Your Favorite Quotations

These next pages are for you to write down your favorite quotations and original lines.

Now this is not the end.
It is not even the beginning of the end.
But it is, perhaps, the end of the beginning.
Winston Churchill

An artist never really finishes his work.
He merely abandons it.

Paul Valéry

All good things must come to an end.
American proverb

*Ends and beginnings—there are no such things.
There are only middles.*

Robert Frost

Nothing is ended with honor which does not conclude better than it began.

Samuel Johnson

That's all there is, there isn't any more.
Ethel Barrymore

Our revels now are ended.
William Shakespeare

That's all folks!

Porky Pig

Index

About the Author

Carol Weston studied French and Spanish comparative literature at Yale and graduated summa cum laude Phi Beta Kappa in 1978. She received her master's in Spanish from Middlebury College in 1979. Carol is the author of *Girltalk: All the Stuff Your Sister Never Told You*, which is still going strong after three editions, thirteen years, and several translations. She also wrote three other books, including *From Here to Maternity*, and she writes the *Help!* column for *Girls' Life* magazine. Her articles, essays, and quizzes have been published in *YM*, *Seventeen*, *Teen*, *Your Prom*, *Glamour*, *Cosmopolitan*, *Redbook*, *Parents*, *Parenting*, *Woman's Day*, *Ladies' Home Journal*, and the *New York Times*. She has been interviewed on National Public Radio's *All Things Considered* and has been a featured guest on television talk shows hosted by Barbara Walters, Oprah Winfrey, Montel Williams, Ricki Lake, Sally Jessy Raphael, Geraldo, and others. Carol lives in Manhattan with her husband, Robert; her daughters, Elizabeth and Emme; and their guinea pig, Pumpkin.